FOREVER,
MIRABELLE

Forever, Mirabelle

SYDNEY WINWARD

Forever, Mirabelle

Cover art by LLewellenDesigns.com

Published by: Silver Forge Books

Trade Paperback 978-1-7374854-9-0

http://www.sydneywinward.com

To all the tomboys who

love to climb trees

and feel the dirt

between their toes.

BOOKS BY SYDNEY WINWARD

The Bloodborn Series

Bloodborn

Bloodbond

Bloodscourge

Bloodbane

Bloodcurse

Sunlight and Shadows Series

A Breath of Sunlight

A Taste of Shadows

A Glimpse of Music

Letters to Love Series

Yours, Sterling

Forever, Mirabelle

Lord Death Series

A Waltz with Lord Death

Novellas

Through Wylder Meadows

Root Brew Float

On Silver Wings

Bloodmoon

Selkie

I

The wealthy had the funds to be whatever they wished. Yet, they all chose to be insufferable boors.

Gilberd Keats glared at the counter, scrubbing and scrubbing with a wet cloth just to keep his hands occupied. He feared he might knock the five churls on their arses if he stopped working for a single second. His father would be put out with him if he started two fights in one month. He'd sworn he wouldn't lose any more customers at the inn.

No matter how hard it proved to be.

The five young men near his own age of twenty-five laughed, the sound obnoxious and loud in the downstairs dining area. One of them waved a hand during a gaudy tale, knocking into his drink. The ale spilled across the table and dripped onto the floor.

Gilberd's jaw clenched, and he scrubbed harder. Harder. Harder.

"Umm…hello!" one of them called out to him across the room. "Aren't you going to clean up this mess?"

He turned his back to them and focused on taking deep breaths to calm himself. *No fights. No fights. No fights.*

"Did you hear me?" The man snapped his fingers. "We don't pay you to stand around."

Fury flashed through him as hot as burned apple pie. He slung the wet cloth over his shoulder and trudged toward the table. Despite the chant in his head, his fists clenched and unclenched. One clean punch would knock the ungrateful piece of curd right on his back.

Just as he reached the table, a hand clamped on his shoulder and squeezed. His father murmured, "I'll take this table. Your mother needs you in the kitchen."

"But—"

"Gil," his father warned.

He turned to find a warning in his father's dark brown eyes, an identical color to his own. But whereas his father's eyes were filled with the weariness of life, Gilberd's still reflected fire and hope for a brighter future.

Someday, he vowed to himself. There had to be more to life than taking orders and cleaning messes.

More snapping fingers. "Old man. Clean it up."

"I'm on it." His father pasted on a practiced smile while he wiped up the spill. "Let me get you another drink, on the house."

No fights. No fights. No fights.

Gilberd passed several tables on his way to the kitchen. Three ladies occupied one of the tables, tittering and giggling behind fancy fans while they wore fancy hats and fancy dresses. At another table was a young peasant family with two tired-looking parents and three excited children bouncing in their seats and running around the dining room.

2

The small town of Millbrook was far from the fanciest town in the kingdom of Edilann, but it was one of the only inns on the road to the palace. They received many high status, well-paying customers. And his father couldn't afford to lose any of them.

He stopped in the doorway separating the space behind the bar from the kitchen, watching as his father graciously took the demands and insults from those five courtly men. Remaining behind the bar tested his restraint.

"Lord Mavis, can I get you anything else?" his father asked with a dip of his head.

"Out of my sight?"

The men laughed. Gilberd stepped forward with fists clenched, but the soft, demure voice of his mother stopped him in his tracks.

"Gil, is that you?"

"Yes." He sighed and backed into the kitchen, casting one final glare at the rowdy table without a speck of manners.

His mother sat at the small table tucked in the corner, dallying with her collection of herbs and medicine. When she wasn't making up rooms, cleaning sheets, or preparing food, she enjoyed making medicine, poultices, and lucky charms in her spare time, mainly to help out the village folk.

What seemed to be a new strand of silver in her brown hair, a shade similar to his, caught a glimmer of light from the open window. Despite growing older and still taking on so many tasks in a day, she always seemed to carry an extra smile in those large pockets she often piled with herbs.

"You're not making trouble again, are you?" she scolded lightly, her back turned to him as she mashed a mixture of herbs together in a mortar.

"I'm not the one making the trouble." To emphasize his point, he gestured in the direction of the dining area. But with her back turned, she didn't see it.

"When you stand near flames, you will likely catch fire." She wiped her hands on a cloth and finally turned to him. "And that fire will spread until everything around you burns."

Gilberd frowned and absently ground his boot into a piece of crusted bread on the floor. When he realized what he'd done, he quickly grabbed a broom to sweep up the crumbs. "What about a sense of justice? How can Father allow others to disrespect him?"

"Gil, my sweet boy, pride doesn't always have to win. Sometimes you must show restraint."

"But did you see how they treated him?"

She fondly rested her hand against his cheek, the comforting touch of a mother. In response to the simple touch, the fire in his soul began to ebb. "You must always be the better man. No matter what someone says or does. You cannot control them. You can only control yourself."

A sigh left his mouth as he moved away from her and busied himself with sweeping the rest of the kitchen. He needed to find the crumbs before the ants did. "I hate how wise you are with these things. Your words make me feel awful. I don't like it."

His mother laughed and returned to her chair at the table. "Then I think my words are working." In the next several moments, she ducked her head to busy herself with a medicine vial. "You are a good man, Gil. Just like your father. No matter what you decide to do with your life."

His brows furrowed at her wording. "I will take over the inn for Father when the time comes."

When she didn't reply immediately, he lifted his head. The bittersweet sadness in her eyes stared back at him, the faintest smile on her lips. Finally, she said, "You were meant for something more than this life. Your father and I have known it for a while now. I am simply reluctant to let you go."

He couldn't help but laugh and shake his head. "There is nowhere for me to go. You needn't worry about losing me."

He was born in Millbrook and would likely die here.

And then he frowned. No matter how much he longed for something more himself.

When he moved to the sink to start washing the dishes from lunch, his mother stepped in front of him with a basket and pressed it into his hands. Several vials of medicine lay within, and she packed a pot of broth and rolls to go with it.

"I have a lot of work to do here," she said, finishing her packing by covering the items with a white cloth. "Will you deliver this to Mr. Waters at the edge of town?"

The woman glanced away from him, but he didn't miss the mischievous curve of her mouth.

"Mother...what are you planning?"

"Nothing." She shrugged. "Mr. Waters' health is failing, and he needs medicine." Pots and pans banged together as she added one after the other to the sink as if to drown out her next words, but he heard them anyway. "And his daughter Mirabelle will be there. I hoped you might make a match of it."

And there it was. A bit of matchmaking mischief.

"Mirabelle Waters?" He laughed at the absurd idea. "The girl who ran around with bare feet and carried a chicken wherever she went?" Braids, dirtied clothing, and defiant eyes came to mind. The boys in town had always teased her

5

growing up. He couldn't recall seeing her in a good while. "Besides, she is four years younger than me."

Mother simply smiled and added one last roll to the basket. "A lot can change within a few years."

Unable to help himself, he laughed again. "Uh huh. We'll see."

She patted him on the cheek and sent him on his way out the kitchen exit. The rambunctious laughter of the mannerless men inside the inn followed him, and he ground his teeth together as he pointedly ignored it. More than once as he traversed the long road leading out of town, he was tempted to turn back for his sword. He felt naked and defenseless without the weapon he'd scrimped and saved for, even trading a few favors for years until he'd purchased it.

But innkeepers weren't supposed to carry weapons, and he didn't want to cast any unnecessary shadows on his parents' establishment.

Homes within the town became farther and farther apart with each passing minute. His boots scuffed against the dirt road as he moved to the side to allow a horse-drawn cart filled with harvested squash to pass. When he continued forward, tall amber grass slowly transitioned to fields of cornstalks and melons. And when several soldiers rode by on horseback, Gilberd stopped to watch them with longing in his eyes.

Metal armor clinked together with each footfall of the horses. The soldiers rode with finesse, masters of their mounts. Swords hung from their waists, shiny pommels glinting beneath the sunlight.

They rounded the bend in the road, out of sight.

A pang echoed in the cavern of his chest. Some men were born to do great things. Others were born to sweep floors and beat rugs.

He tightened his grip on the basket and continued forward. Crop fields transitioned into acres upon acres of green grass for grazing. The Waters' property lay on a large plot of land they used to raise cattle. He turned down the road leading to their home, green grass as tall as his waist brushing against fence posts on either side of him. Dirt and gravel scuffed the bottoms of his shoes, and the scent of livestock and hay greeted each breath.

When he reached the house at the end of the road, several chickens clucked as they darted in front of him followed by an orange barn cat. The feline chased the chickens and pounced but ended up missing. And then as if giving up the chase, it jumped onto the porch railing and stretched in a patch of sunlight.

He placed one foot on the bottom of the stairs but paused when a beautiful sound struck him dumb.

In the distance, a voice rang out, clear and melodic and awe-inspiring like the beat of an angel's wings as it flew over a crystalline sky.

Gilberd retreated from the porch and followed the sound of the angelic song. It led him around the back of the house, along a path surrounded by tall grass, and then he stopped short at the sight of a woman standing on the bottom pegs of a fence, her arms resting on the top.

She continued to sing, each note long but clipped at the end. Cattle lowed as they lumbered in her direction, answering the call with eagerness and loyalty.

But then the song ended when the cows neared the fence where hay lay on the ground for the animals to consume.

As if feeling his eyes on her, the woman spun around to face him.

His lips parted in surprise the moment she turned toward him. Her beauty struck him dumb. Shiny, dark brown tresses brushed against her shoulders. Long, dark eyelashes framed green and brown hazel eyes on a heart-shaped face. His gaze dipped to her slender neck, and then to her clothing. She wore a blue corset over a white blouse that revealed the top of her bare shoulders. A white apron covered blue skirts, and despite the layers, he noticed her nice figure.

"Well?" she asked, her voice as sweet as her song.

Only when she placed her hands on her hips did he realize she'd demanded an answer. He blinked several times, trying to recall what she'd said.

"I'm sorry, repeat that?"

The woman huffed, and a strand of her hair lifted with the breath. "Who are you and why are you here?"

"Oh…um…I…" He cleared his throat and held out the basket. "Gilberd Keats. My mother sent food. And medicine."

Although her hands remained on her hips, her lips slowly lifted in a grin. Her gaze started at his feet, and then followed the length of his body until she met his eye. "Gilberd? Is it really you? I haven't seen you since you cut half of one of my braids off with a knife."

Heat scorched his face, and an itch climbed up his back in the form of guilt. *Please, no. No, no, no! This can't be Mirabelle Waters. No way in kingdom's glory can it be her.* "Nah…I didn't do such a thing. How terrible."

He scratched his lower back, but the itch returned with a vengeance.

The woman ran a lock of her hair between her fingers. "Oh, it was you all right. I will never forget how long it took me to grow out my hair to such a beautiful length, only for a mean bully to destroy it with a small slice of a blade."

"I was not a bully. It was a dare."

"And that changes what you did, how?"

He ran a hand over the coarse hair on his face. He could no longer deny it. This breathtakingly beautiful woman standing before him was the one and only Mirabelle Waters.

He sighed. "I'm so sorry for that."

However, she simply raised a single dark eyebrow as she stared him down. "You tossed my journal into the mud."

"It was—"

"And you also stole the very last bite of my favorite dessert."

"I didn't—"

"Not to mention the time you tossed my book bag into the tree, and I had to climb all the way up to get it back down." Her mouth twitched, and he wasn't sure if it was with anger or amusement. "Would you like me to go on?"

"Ah…" He rubbed the back of his neck. Heat climbed to his ears as he recalled all of the awful things he'd done in his adolescent years. Still, he braved looking into her eyes and tried to hide his embarrassment with flirtation. "You know what they say. Boys tease girls they like."

Her eyebrow lifted higher, the hazel of her eyes scalding. "You are a no-good rascal, Gilberd Keats." On her way past him, she grabbed the basket from his arms. "Thank your mother for me. She has been a wonderful help for my ailing father."

Gilberd watched her moving away, long brown hair swaying to her lower back with each step she took toward her house. And like the fool of a man he was, he couldn't help but follow after something beautiful. Even if it was sharp enough to draw blood.

"Wait!" he called after her, catching up in only a few strides. She was petite and much shorter than him, her head only reaching his chest. "You must remember the time I helped fish you out of the water barrel you fell into."

Out of the corner of her eye, she glared at him. "*You* were the one who pushed me in."

He stumbled in surprise and blinked several times in confusion. "That couldn't have been me. I remember it happening differently."

"Well, it didn't," she snapped.

Tall reeds of grass stopped short at the edge of the dirt path, but before she managed to move any farther, he stepped in front of her. She halted in her tracks, hands on her hips once more while she stared up at him defiantly.

His heart skipped pleasantly. He liked the fire in her eyes. He'd always liked it. It was one of the reasons he'd teased her growing up. That and…

He clamped a hand over his mouth when a laugh attempted to escape. Dainty toes peeked out from the bottom of her dress. Bare. Completely shoeless. He'd been right! Someone couldn't change so much in five years.

"Are you quite finished laughing?" she asked.

Another chuckle escaped him, and he attempted to cover it up with a cough. "I'm not laughing."

A huff. And then she ducked beneath his arm and continued her short journey. A childish part of him wanted to tug on her hair and dodge out of the way of what would usually be her attempt to kick him. Another part of him wanted to sing her ballads and worship the ground she walked on. However, he was terrible at singing and would look ridiculous kissing the ground.

Instead, he followed her again, much to her obvious annoyance. She squared her shoulders and ignored him.

"Where have you been?" he asked, keeping her swaying hair in his sights at all times. "I would have seen you around town."

"Off at school." She rested her basket on the bottom step of the porch and shooed the cat away when it swatted at the cloth. "My father insisted I get an education. But I came home when his condition worsened. I'm here to stay."

She picked up the basket and started toward the door. He placed a foot on the bottom stair, desperate for more conversation. "Will you come with me to the pond tomorrow?"

She scowled at him. "No."

"Have a bite to eat with me at the inn?"

"Also no."

He shrugged his shoulders. "How about a horseback ride? We only have one horse, but I remember how much you love animals."

For a moment, she hesitated. But then her glare returned. "If you think I will go anywhere with you, Gilberd Keats, you are sorely mistaken."

"Then I will come here and help you with the cattle."

The space between them closed with several of her infuriated stomps, but the effect was dwindled by her bare feet. Fire blazed in her eyes, fueling his determination brighter. She had such beautiful eyes. How had he not noticed before? And even though she stood on the top step, he thought he might still be taller than her.

"Do you have no idea what rejection is?" She poked him in the chest. "Is this your new thrill? To bother me until I implode?"

He grimaced. *She hates me.*

But then she smiled, and his heart ceased beating altogether as he stared at the curve of her lips, at the way her entire face lit up. Heat crawled from his toes, up his legs, until his entire chest burst into flames.

At least until he realized she was not smiling at *him*.

The fire in his veins sizzled out at the sight of a lone figure riding up the path on his horse, and the mere glimpse of the man's face boiled his blood once more. What was that insufferable boor doing here?

"Barnaby," Mirabelle said as she descended the steps. "I wasn't sure you would come today."

The other man reined his horse to a stop and hopped to the ground with a dainty thud. He stood much shorter than Gilberd, and while Barnaby was soft with pretty features, Gilberd was a mass of muscle with a harder jaw.

He clenched his fists at his side when Barnaby pulled Mirabelle into an embrace.

And kissed her.

His blood boiled hotter when the man opened his eyes and fixed a stare on him during the kiss, holding tight to Mirabelle even when she tried to pull away. A muffled protest escaped her, and she pushed against his chest. Only then did he release her. She stumbled back several steps, a flush crawling up her neck and into her ears.

"You know I wouldn't miss the chance to see you," Barnaby said, grinning from ear to ear, his expression filled with confidence, victory, and a bit of smugness. The man gasped, but it was completely feigned. "I didn't see you there. Oh, wait." He laughed, mockery dancing in his eyes. "I recognize you. You're the spill-wiper boy who works at the tavern."

Fury clenched his fists tighter. "It's a respectable inn."

"Or do you mean the only inn within miles? I can find much better in another city."

Gilberd's eyes flashed with anger. He pushed up his sleeves and stepped forward, but the man wrapped an arm around Mirabelle's waist and pulled her close, halting him in his tracks. He would gladly pummel the brat into the ground, but he didn't want to hurt Mirabelle by accident.

"Stop it," she murmured to Barnaby.

The man ignored her. Rather, he tightened his grip on her waist. Claiming. Marking his territory.

How long had Barnaby been in town for? Gilberd counted back the days since he and his rowdy friends had bought several rooms at the inn. One week. Could Barnaby possibly have started courting her that quickly?

Despite the confusing messages she sent Barnaby, Mirabelle wasn't protesting any further, nor trying to escape the man's grasp.

Don't start a fight.

His father would lose good-paying customers if he landed his fist in the infuriating man's face. So instead, he dipped his

13

head in farewell, resisting the urge to give the scumbag a finger when Mirabelle wasn't looking. And—

Barnaby slowly lifted a finger of his own, close to his side and away from Mirabelle's line of sight. But plenty noticeable to him.

Gilberd laughed and shook his head, all while his expression said, *Turn your back, and I will kill you.*

The man's only response was to hold Mirabelle tighter.

With hands clenched at his sides, he stalked away before he could do any damage to his family's reputation, and he didn't unclench his fists until he reached the inn. He threw the kitchen door open, startling his mother when it hit the wall with a bang. He pointed a finger to the ceiling to make his point.

"I am going to marry that woman if it's the last thing I do."

M irabelle grimaced as she wiped Barnaby's kiss from her lips for the sixth time. Their first kiss hadn't been unpleasant. But rather awkward, unwanted, and with an audience. Wholly unromantic.

"If you keep doing that," her mother said from where she knitted in her rocking chair beside an unlit hearth, "you will make your lips bleed."

She frowned as she unpacked Papa's medicine from the basket and set it on the simple and scarred wood dining table. They'd had it for as long as she could remember. Her father had built it, and he was still proud of it, even after all these years.

"It embarrassed me," she murmured, resisting the urge to wipe her lips again. "I never thought a kiss should feel embarrassing."

"It shouldn't." Her mother leveled her with a stare over her spectacles. "Unless you are kissing the wrong man."

"Ha!" She rolled her eyes. "What other men are there? I don't exactly have a line of suitors in Millbrook." At school in the bigger city, she'd had plenty of suitors. Now in this small little town, she felt awkward and small and invisible as she had in her youth.

"Two makes a line."

At first, her eyebrows furrowed. And then she spun around so fast that the action gave her a sudden headache. "You don't mean Gilberd."

"I do." Mama tucked a strand of dark gray hair behind her ear. "He's a good man, August Keats' son."

"Gilberd?" She scoffed and turned her back to make her father a plate from Mrs. Keats' generous gift. "You do realize I dedicated a diary to my hatred of that boy."

Mama chuckled and waved her knitting needle in her direction. "I remember he loved teasing you. But it has been five years since the two of you have seen each other."

"And thank the river for that. He was a terror." The plate scraped against the table when she moved it to the side to make room for the medicine. "He cut off my hair, Mama!"

Finally, her mother sighed as she set aside her ball of yarn and rocked back and forth in her chair. "Don't you remember that day? I know you were upset, but he brought a letter by to apologize."

"I never opened it." In fact, she hadn't left her room in three days after the incident. "Besides, he made my life miserable."

Mama chuckled. "So does every boy to the girl they like, at least until they mature and do things properly."

She exasperatedly pressed her palms flat on the table. "Four-year age gap, Mama. Don't even suggest he liked me. He's so much older."

"Your father is eight years older than I am."

"And Barnaby is only two years older." But even as she said it, the feel of his lips against hers worked another cringe up her spine, and she turned her mouth into her shoulder to wipe it on her sleeve. Why had he chosen that moment to kiss her? She wanted to be romanced. Not taken by surprise at a bad time.

"I just want to see you married," her mother croaked, wincing at the pain coursing through her joints. "Preferably happily married. You will need someone to support you. And soon."

Tears burned Mirabelle's eyes as she held Papa's medicine tighter.

Her mother continued. "You should have accepted that lad's proposal from Edilann. He was wealthy. Educated. A good match."

Jaw clenching and unclenching, she replied, "Two things. He was forty years old. Nearly twice my age! And I'd hate more than anything to be caged. I want to let my hair down. Feel the dirt between my toes. Ride through the meadows as fast as I want."

For a moment, as her mother stared back at her, she thought she would tell her she had to change. To grow up. To become a proper lady.

But Mama only offered the barest hint of a smile. "Then you will need to find someone who will accept you as you are, and not try to conform you to what they want you to be." And then she returned her attention to her knitting.

Those words echoed in her mind, pounding ceaselessly against her skull. She picked up the plate of food and medicine and ventured into her father's room.

Darkness.

The stiff air stifled her lungs. Drawing breath became difficult. The scent of mint, lavender, and sickness permeated the room, covering every inch of space from the thick drapes to the bedside table stacked with used bowls to worn wooden floors.

Papa lay on the bed, eyes closed and skin pale. Raspy breaths escaped his mouth, occasional winces finding his expression in sleep. Guilt pounded in her stomach, tossing and turning and tossing some more. She wanted more than anything for him to stay alive. To heal. To become healthy again. She also wanted him to die. To no longer feel the pain of his sickness. To be free.

"Papa," she murmured, gently shaking his shoulder until he stirred.

He blinked several times, groggily glancing about the room as if it was filled with bright light until his gaze landed on her. "My little angel," he wheezed.

Her eyes smarted at his tender greeting, and to distract her thoughts, she began tearing a roll into smaller bites and helping him eat. He chewed slowly, eyes unfocused. His soul barely hung on by a thread to his body like a baby tooth ready to snap off one's gums. The faintest of breezes just might break the remaining thread.

"Barnaby came by again today," she said, making conversation.

"Who?"

"Barnaby Mavis, remember? I met him in town a week ago."

All too suddenly, Papa stopped chewing and stared back at her. The briefest flicker of life entered his eyes as if parts of

18

his soul tried to cling onto his body. "Mavis? The son of Lord Mavis?"

She shrugged. "I suppose so." Though she'd heard someone call Barnaby "Lord Mavis" and assumed his father might have passed and he'd inherited the title.

He turned his head and winced, and then squeezed his eyes shut. "What did he want?"

"Well…" Warmth settled in her face, and she was glad he still closed his eyes as to not witness her fluster. "To court me."

A long pause. Long enough that she thought he fell asleep. But then he sighed. "Forgive me, my beautiful Mirabelle. For this position I've put you in." He coughed, his lungs violently rattling with each hack.

"Shh," she reassured and helped him sit just enough to drink tepid water to soothe his throat. "You have nothing to apologize for."

"But I do," he wheezed. "I am in so much debt."

Mirabelle jerked upright in shock, eyes staring hard at her father. But his eyelids only fluttered closed, his chest rising and falling with slow, labored breaths.

Debt? What debt?

She poked her head out of the room, her gaze finding her mother still sitting with her knitting. A lump of dread formed in her throat when she realized *what* the clacking of her knitting needles created. A death scarf. The purest of white yarn formed a long tail on her lap. Soon, instead of resting in her lap, the priestess in town would bless it and it would tie her father's body to heaven.

"Mama," she rasped. "Are you and Papa in debt?"

Her needles stopped momentarily before continuing their fluid movements. "Did your father say that? You know he has been somewhat delirious. We're not in debt. We have a nice house. A herd of cattle. We are thriving. And we will continue to make it."

Thankfully, her mother's words helped soothe her worries. But as she glanced back at her father, she frowned. Had he been delirious? Or was he truly indebted to someone?

No. She straightened her spine before returning outside to feed the chickens. It would be absurd if they were in debt. Her father had made a good living off raising cattle. And with or without a husband, she would, too.

Clang!

The blow of sword against sword reverberated down Gilberd's arm as he sparred one on one with his older brother while Jeremy's wife, Camilla, played with the children on the green, manicured lawn beside several rows of flowers.

He pushed his brother away before they clashed together once more. Strike. Strike. Block! Both of their bare torsos contained a sheen of perspiration, each of them breathing heavily after an hour of sparring beneath the warm rays of summer sunshine.

When Jeremy charged at him, Gilberd side-stepped and twisted the weapon out of the other man's grip, sending it flying through the air. It landed on the flattened grass and lay still. He won. Again.

"You are getting rusty, old man," Gilberd commented. He stooped to pick up the sword he had disarmed from his brother and handed it back, each of them with perspiration dripping down their faces.

"Rusty? Old man?" Jeremy laughed, swiping the sweat from his face with his equally sweaty arm. "I am only six years older than you."

"Which puts you in your thirties. Is that gray in your hair?"

Jeremy lashed out with a kick to his knee, but he expertly dodged the attack, laughing as they made their way toward a stone bench with their clothing and equipment.

"But in all seriousness…" Jeremy wiped his face with a quickly dirtying cloth. "What are you still doing at the inn? Why not work as a guardsman or a soldier in the king's army?" He pointed at him. "You've wanted to be a soldier all your life."

He shrugged, and instead of cleaning up, he climbed onto an overhanging branch of a tree behind the inn and flipped upside down. With his hands behind his head, he began his next exercise of touching his elbows to his knees. He needed to be in top shape for…

For what? Sweeping floors and making beds? He was a tall, muscular man who stood out like a black bean in potato soup.

"Our parents got into a financial bind." Elbow, knee. Elbow, knee. "They couldn't hire anyone to help. They didn't want to ask you. And I would feel terrible if I left them without help now."

Jeremy grimaced. "I suppose my decision to move to Armandy had been a selfish one."

From his upside-down position, Gilberd studied his brother. He was different. Older, to be sure. But his voice contained a different accent from spending years overseas, with twice-yearly visits to Edilann to visit the family.

"You found a wife," he grunted, the exertion of the exercise becoming more difficult with each set. "And you have two children. It's not selfish to take care of them."

"But I left you to take care of our parents on your own."

A grin spread across his face. "Don't let Ma hear you say that. She'll say—"

"—she can handle her own better than both of us combined." They laughed together. "Says we're both helpless without a woman in our lives."

"At least you have one," Gilberd pointed out and continued in a teasing, self-mocking tone, "At this rate, I'll be helpless forever."

Jeremy sat and pulled his shirt over his head, but not before returning his wife's coy glance. And when Gilberd snorted teasingly, Jeremy punched him in the arm. "Ma told me about that Annabelle girl."

"Mirabelle," he corrected. "Not only does she hate me," he grunted with the effort of the exercise, "but she is also courting someone else. If you have any tips, I'd really appreciate you sharing them with me."

His brother shrugged. "I don't know. Flowers?"

Before he had a chance to reply, his nieces ran across the lawn toward them, brown braids flying behind them and skirts swishing with each excited footstep. "Uncle Gil! Uncle Gil!" The oldest, Heather, tripped over her own shoe but righted herself just as quickly. "Do that trick when you close your eyes."

"Please?" Samantha asked, batting her eyelashes at him. At four years old, the girl was the cutest little manipulative stinker.

"Fine," he chuckled, pausing upside down for a moment to take in the scenery before him. Green grass. Leafy trees. Garden bench. Watering pot. Stacked crates. He paid special attention to the girls' hair and clothing and then closed his eyes, counting down slowly. "Five. Four. Three. Two. One."

When he opened his eyes, everything appeared to be the same. Everything except...

"You took the ribbon out of your hair," he commented, gesturing to Heather.

The girls exclaimed excitedly while his brother shook his head. "How do you do that?" Jeremy asked. "Your memory is incredible."

Gilberd shrugged. At least as much as he could while hanging upside down. He continued the exercise. Only a few more and he'd be finished. "The skill comes in handy once in a while."

"Again! Again!" the girls cried in unison.

This time, he counted down from twenty, and when he opened his eyes, his heart nearly lurched out of his chest at the figure standing before him, a hand on her hip. Brown hair. Hazel eyes. The sweetest glare.

"Mirabelle!" he gasped.

Gilberd fell right out of the tree and landed on his side, while simultaneously, his older brother, Jeremy Keats, ushered two girls toward the inn.

For a moment, all Mirabelle managed to do was stare at Gilberd as he scrambled to his feet. Her mouth formed an "o" shape, her gaze roaming over his broad shoulders, the burly muscles of his arms, the hardness of his chest. His abdominal muscles were each defined, tapering off at an attractive, sturdy waist.

Heat traveled from her feet, up her legs, and then it nestled in her cheeks. All this time, she never realized his shirt hid *that*. Oh, he was so very attractive. And she hated it.

Pulling her gaze away from his torso to his face proved difficult, and despite his previous fluster, a characteristic grin now pulled on his mouth.

She held tighter onto the basket in her arms, refraining from allowing her gaze to slip when it threatened to waver.

"I came to find your mother, but instead I found you. How fortunate for me." Her voice leaked sarcasm.

He ignored her gibe and smirked at her feet. "You're wearing shoes today."

Yes, because she never ventured away from home without them. No matter how much they bothered her. "Better for kicking your behind with. Stay away from our ranch."

"I can't promise that." He leaned a shoulder against the tree, studying her with serious yet mirthful eyes. "Will you go to a barn raising with me next week?"

"Over my dead body."

"To the market?"

"Never."

His smile grew wider across his face. "Stand next to a tree and talk?"

She scowled at him. "I came to give this back." She stepped closer, but her self-control wavered, and her gaze dipped once more to his bare chest. However, judging by the unrepentant grin growing across his face, he noticed.

A raging blush filled her cheeks, and she shoved the basket into his arms. But when she began to stalk away, he called after her.

"Wait! You'll wake them up."

Huh? She stopped in her tracks and slowly turned back to face him, only to find him shrugging a shirt over his head and hiding the distracting brawn from her view. He placed a finger to his lips and pointed to the boughs of the tree above him.

With furrowed brows, she mouthed, *What's up there?*

He mouthed back, *You'll just have to see.*

Without another wasted second, he hefted himself onto the bottom branch with hardly a sound, making the action appear effortless. For a moment, she stood rooted to the spot and overcome with uncertainty. A part of her warned her to stride away from him with what remained of her dignity. The curious part of her wanted to follow.

At last, she kicked off her shoes and stood at the base of the tree, hands on her hips as she contemplated how to climb it. Gilberd was approximately a foot taller than her and brawny to boot. Her, on the other hand… She was small and petite. If she could just find a stool—

A hand appeared in front of her face, momentarily taking her off guard. She glared at the hand, then at the person it belonged to. "You are daft if you think I will take your hand," she hissed at him. But he only placed a finger to his mouth again, continuing to offer his aid.

The last person she wanted help from was the horrid man before her, but she wanted to know what slept within the confines of the branches.

"Don't you dare drop me, Keats," she said quietly.

"I wouldn't dream of it," he murmured back.

And then she took a firm grasp of his hand. In a surprisingly strong and agile movement, he heaved her onto the branch next to him. She gripped his arm tight, seeking balance. The warmth from his body seeped into her, which seemed to transfer to her face as she glanced up at him. Their gazes locked. Twin pools of brown mimicked the deep colors of the forest in his eyes. Constant. Steady. Captivating.

Her stomach tumbled with treacherous nerves, dancing and spinning and rolling with a strange, unfamiliar, and even unwelcome heat.

She broke eye contact and steadied herself against a branch rather than his arm. *He once put a snail down the back of my dress,* she reminded herself, and her indifference returned with a vengeance.

Slowly, and with as little noise as possible, she climbed after him, following his path through the branches. At least until he stopped halfway up the tree and pointed to something on his left.

What are you gesturing to, Gilberd? she asked in her mind. All she saw were brown branches, green leaves, and—

Oh!

Excitement pattered in her chest when she noticed the bundle of carefully crafted twigs, cotton, and loose threads. Her fingers clasped around rough branches, and velvety leaves caressed her face as she climbed higher until she found herself face to face with three feathery baby birds huddled together within their nest.

Her eyes widened and her breath hitched. They were so small! Not yet ready to leave the nest, the birds sported clusters of feathers, eyes still closed in their youth. One of them stretched their small wings before snuggling with its siblings.

She couldn't remember the last time she'd seen a nest filled with baby birds. The barn cat on the property often chased the creatures away, and she hadn't seen any nests while going to school in the bigger city.

Warmth hugged her heart. A simple kindness from who she used to think of as her arch nemesis. She lifted her gaze to find Gilberd watching not the birds, but *her*. His mouth lifted in a half-smile. Not a smirk. No teasing notes in his eyes. He genuinely cared.

Her gaze slid toward the nest once more and then to her bare feet. Her mother's words echoed in her mind.

"Then you will need to find someone who will accept you as you are, and not try to conform you to what they want you to be."

She shut that door faster than chickens pecking up their morning breakfast. Gilberd was the last person she would *ever* marry. Not just because of the age gap, but because of how many tears she'd cried behind closed doors while growing up. In the past, she'd pretended to have emotions made of steel. But his constant teasing had hurt.

"You locked me in the broom closet at church when I was eleven!" she blurted, a little too loudly, as the birds startled awake and began chirping hungrily for their mother.

27

A grimace replaced his previously warm smile. "I…uh…" He cleared his throat, averting his gaze as he fiddled with his sleeve. "My friends—"

"—dared you to do it, didn't they?" With a hand on her hip and the other keeping her steady on a branch, she glared at him. She felt like she was eleven years old again rather than twenty-one.

"Well…yes…" Although he still refused to look at her, he fussed even more with his sleeve. "They dared me to kiss you. I got scared. And, well, the broom closet was a safer bet."

"Kiss?" Her heart hammered in both fluster and surprise, and her hand fell from her hip to her side. Involuntarily, her gaze dropped to his lips, but she pulled it back up to witness the guilt in his eyes. "I don't believe it. You left me in there for an *hour*! The priestess ended up finding me."

He flinched at her words. "Not my finest moment. I truly am sorry for that."

The man's apology disarmed her, and the barbed words on her tongue dissolved into sugar. "I was four years younger than you."

He shrugged and picked at a nearby leaf, absently shredding it into pieces. "You were cute."

The confession spun her mind in circles, making her dizzy until she steadied her back against the branch behind her. Mama couldn't possibly be right about boys making the lives of the girls they liked miserable. At least until they matured enough to do things properly. The logic made no sense. No sense at all.

"An *hour*, Keats," she repeated. "In the dark."

Another grimace. "I suppose I could have done things differently."

"Yes, you could have."

That smirk of his returned when he finally met her gaze, and she mentally braced herself for what might come out of his mouth. "Like locking myself in there with you."

"You are impossible," she growled, pulling back a branch and whacking him in the arm before she began clambering back down the tree. The moment her feet hit the ground, she glanced up at him. "Besides!" she shouted, followed by her own little smirk. "I would never have allowed you to kiss me."

His laughter followed her long after she slipped her shoes back on and left the property, leaving the basket behind. The faintest warmth of fondness lit the kindling in her heart.

And she didn't know what to make of it.

"I have the finest collection of daggers, second only to the king himself," Barnaby gloated, Mirabelle's hand tucked into the crook of his elbow. They walked side by side, perusing the stands of goods at the market. Fruits. Vegetables. Weapons. Hand-crafted items. "When I see a beautiful thing, I can't help but make it mine."

The man winked at her. No reaction within her accompanied his words. No fluttering stomach. No pounding heart. Rather than walking on a cloud, she was overly aware of the rolling carts, the dusty air, the haggling customers, and the stifling afternoon heat.

Barnaby stopped in front of a booth filled with gold and silver jewelry. Necklaces. Bracelets. Precious gems. And when he faced her, tension tightened in her gut. He gazed down at her, several good inches shorter than Gilberd. And his eyes were a light blue, nothing like Gilberd's deep, soulful brown eyes.

Why am I thinking about that big bully?

Panic increased the tension within her body until every thread of emotion was pulled tight enough to snap. He leaned closer. She froze. But instead of kissing her in a market full of bustling people, he lifted his hand and tucked a strand of hair behind her ear.

"It fell out of its bun," he explained, followed by a grin. A possession lingered in his eyes, as if he knew he already had her within his grasp.

Mirabelle released a tense breath, a hand over her churning belly. *I don't know if I want this.*

But why wouldn't she? Papa's health was declining, and she owed it to her mother to find some way to help support the two of them. The easiest way was to find a husband. And fast. The least she could do was try. Barnaby was a wealthy man with wealthy friends and a secure position at court. What more could she want?

"You look a bit faint," he commented. "Like I said yesterday, you're getting too much sun." He touched a freckle just over her eyebrow, a disapproving frown on his face. "I have a surprise for you. Go wait in the shade for a minute, will you?"

Not knowing how to reply, she simply nodded and walked away from the booth, dodging a donkey pulling a cart piled with apples. She approached a shady tree beside another booth filled with colorful, fashionable scarves. But then she paused when she caught sight of the mirror tipped upward to reveal her reflection. The older woman who owned the booth paid her little heed, fanning herself against the heat of the sun.

Slowly, she moved closer to the mirror and frowned. She had very few freckles on her face, but Barnaby didn't seem to care for them. Several strands of chestnut locks had fallen out of her bun, now framing her face and tickling the back of her neck. A scar lay on her jaw just below her ear from when a horse's hoof had nicked her years ago. And her lips were chapped from licking them too many times in this relentless heat.

If she chose to eventually marry Barnaby, how much would he and his acquaintances judge her imperfections? Did she belong as a lady at court?

Uncertainty leaked across her features when she glanced down at her feet. Shoes hid the dirt between her toes, and the hem of her dress concealed the scratches on her ankles she'd received from weeding the front garden.

Surely, Barnaby would disapprove of that as well.

Loud laughter startled her from her troubling thoughts, and she spun around to find Gilberd with his mother. He followed her around the market, holding a crate filled to the brim with a variety of fruits, vegetables, cheeses, and other ingredients. The man stuck out from the crowd, his brawny bulk a pleasing beacon to the eye.

When his mother said something Mirabelle couldn't discern from this distance, he huffed and rolled his eyes, but the moment she turned her back, he smiled softly. And she found herself smiling as well. He clearly loved his mother.

"Gilberd, come grab these for me," Mrs. Keats said, gesturing to a booth filled with herbs, particularly to a bunch hanging too high for her to reach.

He set the crates on the ground and followed after, and he continued to leave them abandoned when she led him to another booth out of sight.

Two small boys peeked their heads around a vacant cart before darting toward the crates. To her shock, they each dug into its contents, filled their arms with food, and then darted away again before she could call after them.

She rushed toward the crate in an attempt to stop any other thieving from taking place, but when she searched the vicinity for Gilberd, he was gone.

"You are just going to leave it here?" she muttered to herself, hands on her hips. "In the open? Unsupervised?"

No one answered her question, but she didn't expect anyone to either. She stooped down and tried to lift the crate, but to her immense shock, it was so heavy that she couldn't even lift it an inch. She tried again, muscles straining against her efforts, but its weight seemed to nail it to the ground.

"Blasted…Gilberd…" she grunted, attempting the feat one more time without success. "Stronger than you look."

"Should I take offense to that?"

Her head shot up, but then heat scalded her face when she found herself nose to nose with the man in question. A spark lit Gilberd's expression, and he flashed her a bright smile. The warmth in her face turned into an inferno.

As quickly as possible, she straightened and put distance between them. He rose as well from his crouched position but still left the crate on the ground. His grin lingered on his face. Bright. Breathtaking. Far too adorable.

She squashed the thought and tried hard to prevent her gaze from dropping to his mouth. For a moment, she searched her memories for something awful he had done in the past, but the feat proved more difficult than usual.

Ha! He licked a candy and stuck it in my hair. Took forever to get it free.

"You had some little thieves," she said, defending herself.

Yet, his expression transitioned into amusement. He didn't seem to be alarmed at the information.

"Those children are from the orphanage," he said, nodding his head toward the two boys peeking their heads around the empty cart, mouths stuffed with apples. "We've invited them to the inn for a free meal every day. Some days they come. Some days they don't. They didn't come today. Thought to let them help themselves to the food in here." He nodded toward the crate on the ground.

Her lips parted in surprise, and she couldn't help but look at him in a different light—a light free from past prejudices and hatred.

"Gilberd. That's…" She blinked back the surprise in her eyes. This wasn't the same Gilberd she had harbored in the dark recesses of her memory. Was it? "I don't know what to say. You are thoughtful and generous."

He simply shrugged and didn't comment, but she swore his ears turned a light shade of pink.

His intense gaze held hers for several long moments. "Will you go to the creek with me today?"

"So you can push me in?" Slowly, her eyebrow raised in a challenging stare.

"Never. I remember you can't swim. But the water would feel nice. It's a hot day."

The instant refusal died on her tongue, and a strange sense of disappointment fell over her. She pulled her gaze away from him and stared at a lone pebble buried in the dirt while rubbing a hand over her elbow. "I can't. Barnaby is treating me to dinner."

Tension charged the following silence.

"Well," he shrugged, "*can't* is better than *won't* this time around. I'll take it." He bent over his crate. "I have something for you. Even better that you're at the market as well."

34

He pulled out a small bouquet of wildflowers. Her breath caught when he handed them to her. An array of pink, purple, blue, and white petals shimmered beneath the sunlight.

They were beautiful.

Yet, her past interactions with him made her wary. She turned them between her fingers and inspected the bouquet for bugs, poison ivy, or an excess amount of pollen. Nothing out of the ordinary stood out.

"What are these for?"

Stooping down to pick up the crate with relative ease, he grinned. "I am determined to court you. If my intentions haven't been blatantly obvious, I suppose I need to try better."

"There you are," a voice behind her made her jump, and she spun around to face Barnaby's accusatory stare. "You weren't where you said you'd be."

I didn't say anything at all.

But she didn't want to voice the argument.

Barnaby and Gilberd stared at each other, hostility in their eyes. Heat seemed to crackle through the air, mixed with uncomfortable tension.

"Spill-wiper," Barnaby greeted.

Mirabelle watched as Gilberd clenched his fists around the crate, relaxed them, and clenched them once more. In tandem, his mouth opened and closed as if he were trying to find the right words to reply.

But before he could, his mother approached and touched a hand to his back. "Let's get this to the kitchen so we can start cooking for the dinner rush."

The tension buzzed faster. Louder. Yet, he nodded. "See you around, Mirabelle."

She watched him turn away, but not before Mrs. Keats cast a glance at her, then at Barnaby. That simple look... It caused shame to crawl up her neck and shoulders.

Shame for what? She hadn't done anything wrong.

"Give me those." Barnaby snatched the bouquet of wildflowers from her hand and threw them into the dirt. Horror grew in her eyes as he ground his boot into the flowers, tearing the gentle petals to pieces until brown muddied the precious colors.

Slowly, she lifted her gaze as anger bubbled up inside her, rolling like acid in her stomach. "Why would you do that? It was a kind gift."

"And so is mine." He slipped a silver bracelet onto her wrist, the cold metal biting against her skin. "Besides, you have no business with the spill-wiper boy. You are far too beautiful for this town, Mirabelle. You deserve pretty ball gowns and court luxury and to be the most beautiful woman flaunted in Edilann. Someone like Spill-wiper?" He raised a perfectly arched blond eyebrow. "He will never get anywhere. He is too poor and uneducated."

Nearly every word from his mouth rubbed her the wrong way. *Luxury. Flaunted. Poor. Uneducated.*

"His name is Gilberd," she said hoarsely.

"And his is Nathaniel." He gestured to an older gentleman with copper hair and mustache at a produce booth, who most certainly *wasn't* Nathaniel. The man's name was Ted. "A gem like you will only shine in the right lighting."

Despite all of the people weaving around them as they stood in the middle of the road, Mirabelle remained rooted to the spot, staring back at him as she tried to comprehend his words. Surely, no one would say such things. At least not out loud. But he spoke them without shame.

"You think I can't shine here."

"I didn't necessarily say that. I know how the men in this town talk about you. You've caught just about every eye in Millbrook." When she opened her mouth to protest, he quickly interrupted. "With just a little refining, you will shine brighter in Edilann."

Each one of her blemishes and imperfections crashed down on her, leaving behind a puddle of insecurity. She hugged her arms closer to her, wondering just how much he found wrong with her. Would any woman be perfect enough for him? She wasn't. And she realized she didn't want to be.

Braving looking him in the eye, she attempted to stand taller despite the churning anxiety within her. "You know what? This isn't going to work, Barnaby."

His jaw clenched, and his eyes flashed with dangerous fire. When his fist balled at his side, she took a step backward, afraid he might strike her, even in a crowded marketplace. But instead, he grabbed her wrist and yanked her closer until she bumped against his chest. The mere contact sent a flurry of anxious nerves through her stomach.

He lowered his mouth to her ear. "I just bought you a nice, *expensive* gift. The least you could do is accompany me to dinner."

The word "no" lay on the tip of her tongue, but it refused to work in its petrified state. Instead, her gaze darted to his balled fist once again. In her momentary distraction, he pulled her along beside him, his grip tight on her arm.

She just had to get through dinner. After that, she didn't know what she would do.

M irabelle's gaze darted toward the road for the hundredth time that day, terrified she might catch a glimpse of blond hair and ice blue eyes. Although Barnaby had been cordial and sickeningly sweet to her during dinner last night, she feared he might show up at any moment.

Even as evening approached.

She arched her aching back as she stood from the stool beside the cow, finishing the last of the milking. Her fingers stiffened with pain. The backs of her hands were cracked and bleeding. And several new blisters burned the tips of her fingers and palms.

A sob climbed her throat. She forced it back down.

Her weary body swayed as she set the pail aside and leaned heavily against the door of the barn, staring out at absolute chaos. Weeds crawled across the ground, often getting caught in the horse's hooves and the cattle's horns. Chicken feathers lay scattered across the gravel because the coop had a hole in it and a fox had gotten inside. Two apple trees stretched toward the waning sunlight in a tangle of limbs and festering branches. It had been years since they'd been properly pruned.

The rumble in her stomach reminded her she hadn't eaten anything since last night. With so much to do on the property, she'd forgotten.

Pink, orange, and yellow streaks across the sky blurred in her vision. She sniffed and pushed her emotions away. But when her gaze darted toward the empty road in front of the property, a new anxiety cut through her. She couldn't keep living in fear like this. She had to tell Barnaby to stay away from her once and for all.

After drafting a hasty letter and placing it, along with the silver bracelet, into the pocket of her apron, she slipped her shoes on and winced when they rubbed against the blisters on her feet. Her eyelids drooped as she trudged down the long stretch of road leading into town.

The aching muscles in her legs felt heavy, as if she found herself moving through sludge. And the back of her neck was sticky with perspiration. How long had she been working today?

Since the rooster crowed this morning.

At last, the town came into view, the flickering lantern lights guiding her way until she stood in front of the inn. Loud laughter and conversation from within caused her heart to race with panic. She didn't want to face Barnaby. She was scared.

Still, she pushed the door open and stepped into the dim interior. Nearly every table was full with patrons drinking ale and consuming a supper consisting of meat and vegetable stew. But instead of growling with hunger, her stomach protested with churning sickness at the thought of an inevitable confrontation.

She scanned the room for Barnaby, but to her relief and disappointment, he wasn't there. And if she admitted as much to herself, she couldn't see a head of brown hair belonging to a tall and strapping man either.

Across the room, Mrs. Keats caught her eye from where she stood behind the counter. Rowdy laughter and faint harmonica music followed her path toward the woman. Alarm flitted across the woman's features upon looking at her, but before she opened her mouth, Mirabelle spoke first.

"I don't know what room Barnaby is staying in." She slipped the bracelet and envelope out of her pocket and handed it to Mrs. Keats. "Can you get this to him?" She swallowed. "I don't want to face him."

Mrs. Keats pulled her closer to the kitchen and asked where the noise wasn't so loud, "May I ask why?"

Mirabelle knew she should say nothing, to not create problems and involve people who didn't need to get involved. But the other woman's hand was warm and comforting on her shoulder, and her eyes were understanding and kind.

"He makes me feel like I can't say no." Tears once again blurred her vision. She wiped her eyes with her palm. "I don't feel…safe."

"Oh, honey…" Mrs. Keats gently took a hold of her hand and pulled her out of the room and into the back of the kitchen. A man she recognized as Gilberd's older brother glanced up, along with his wife who stirred a pot of stew on the stove. Their gazes trailed their path to a table tucked into the corner of the room where Mrs. Keats proceeded to guide her into a chair. In moments, a steaming bowl of stew and a large glass of water sat before her.

Her emotions wavered, becoming more and more difficult by the second to keep them at bay. "I don't have any money."

The woman sat beside her and patted her cracked hand, crusted with flecks of dried blood. "You, Mirabelle, will never be charged. Why don't you eat and tell me what's weighing on your heart."

"But…" Glancing behind her, she found the other two now focused on their culinary tasks while Mr. Keats walked in and out with empty dishes or steaming plates. "You are so busy here."

"And I have two new helpers for the next week. We'll manage."

More than anything, she wanted to shovel the food into her mouth and quell her rumbling stomach. But instead, tears spurted from her eyes and sobs escaped as relentless waves. This woman was so kind. For weeks, she had felt so alone. The last person she expected to listen to her was Gilberd's *mother.*

"Ha!" Gilberd shouted in triumph as he burst into the kitchen, holding up his bounty—a large wheel of cheese. "I made it in the nick of time. He even cut me a discount—"

He stopped short at the sight of familiar brown hair, a heart-shaped face, and hazel eyes filled to the brim with tears.

Mirabelle dabbed her red-rimmed eyes on her apron, but as if she couldn't stop them, the tears kept coming.

His focus solely on her, he set the cheese aside and strode toward her. His heart ached at the sight of her tears. He wanted to take them away. By any means necessary.

"Gil," his mother warned. "Now isn't the best time."

"Who made you cry?" He dropped into the chair on the opposite side of her. "I will knock them flat on their arse." If it was Barnaby, he would wring the man's neck and make sure he sported two black eyes into the middle of next year.

She opened her mouth as if to reply, but all that managed to escape were sobs. His mother gathered her in her arms and rocked her as she cried like she had done for him when he'd been a child.

Finally, Mirabelle blubbered through her sobs and tears. "I am so tired. So overwhelmed." A sob. A hiccup. More eye wiping. "I'm scared of losing my father. My mother's joints are so stiff that she can't help on the ranch." Muffled sobs as his mother held her closer. "I can't keep up with the chores. There is so much to do. My whole body aches. My hands hurt."

Gilberd reached for her hand, surprised when she let him, and turned it over so her palm faced him. His stomach tightened at the sight of blisters and bleeding cracks. Without a word, he stood and gathered a bowl of water, a cloth, salve, and bandages from his mother's collection at her medicine table. She still didn't protest when he began to gently wipe away the blood and dirt on her skin. A wince of pain contorted her beautiful features, and he tried to be even gentler with her injuries.

42

"You don't have any help?" his mother asked quietly, and Mirabelle shook her head.

"Papa refuses to give me permission to sell the cattle. He won't allow me to hire anyone either." Several sniffs took the place of her previously relentless sobs. "My parents are pressuring me to marry before my father dies." She wiped her eyes again. "I don't want to marry Barnaby. He isn't very kind."

He paused halfway into wrapping her hand with a bandage. "What did that horse snot do to you?" he growled.

A shrug lifted her shoulders, and she sniffed again. Loud dishes clattered in the sink as Jeremy began to wash bowls and plates. Camilla, glanced over at them, concern in her brows.

"Nothing terrible," she finally answered. "I don't like the way he treats me."

Gilberd frowned as he finished wrapping her hand. It wasn't his place to tell her about the lewd comments Barnaby often made about women, nor about the women he'd brought up to his room at the inn. In all honesty, he feared the man might try to pressure or coerce Mirabelle into such a situation. If he hadn't already.

"Has he hurt you?" he asked, his voice dangerously quiet.

"No."

After he finished the wrapping, he kept his fingers resting over hers. He didn't know what comfort he could possibly offer her, but there was something he *could* do.

"Ma, if I take a few days off, will the four of you be able to handle the inn without me?"

"You aren't the *only* person managing to keep us afloat," she teased, pinching his arm. "Even if you *are* the only person who is strong enough to move the beds and tables for cleaning."

He chuckled. "Jeremy is plenty strong. You don't give him enough credit." Sincerity lay within the depths of his expression as he returned Mirabelle's gaze. Such lovely eyes. Even with a face smudged with dirt and puffy eyes from crying, she was beautiful. "I'm yours for the next few days then, Mirabelle. When I come by tomorrow morning, I expect you to have a list ready for me for all of your harder chores."

She stared back at him with wide eyes. Her lips parted in surprise. "W-w-what?"

"A list." He grinned, amused at the bewildered look on her face. "Chores. You know, like milking cows and hefting hay. Ma always has me lifting the heavy things. You can start with that."

After several long moments, Mirabelle covered her face with her hand, and then her shoulders began shaking silently. He and his mother shared a look of worry. Sympathy. Concern. How long had Mirabelle shouldered these responsibilities in silence? Without complaint? Without help?

Crash! Shatter! Thunk!

"Gilbie!" Jeremy called several moments later as he peered around the corner, using his childhood nickname. "Huge mess on table four. The kid climbed up. Toppled the entire thing. Water. Glass. Stew. You name it."

"Ugh," he muttered under his breath as he stood from his chair and slapped a cloth over his shoulder. "I really am the spill-wiper boy. At least it wasn't on purpose this time."

He glanced back at the table to find his mother rubbing soothing circles on Mirabelle's back while she continued to cover half her face with one hand and spooned stew into her mouth with the other.

"Don't leave the inn without me," he said, pointing to Mirabelle. "I can't let you walk back home in the dark by yourself."

Not waiting for her answer, he strode out of the kitchen and scanned the dining area. The bawling child led his gaze toward the now-righted table, but everything that had previously rested on top now lay scattered on the floor beneath it. He grabbed a broom and dustpan, and then approached two parents trying to console one of their children.

"We are so sorry," the father apologized, reaching for the broom, but Gilberd shook his head.

"It happens." As he swept, he addressed the crying child, who clung tight around his mother's neck. "Do you like climbing things?"

The boy sniffed, nodding into the woman's shoulder.

"You must be good at climbing trees then. I know someone with an adventurous spirit, just like you. You would get along well with her."

The small child's tears ceased, and he offered a flicker of a smile but no more as Gilberd finished cleaning the mess. But then the hairs on the back of his neck raised like hackles the moment the front door slammed open and several drunk, gaudy men stumbled inside.

One of them was Barnaby.

His jaw clenched as he watched the men bully a family out of their chairs and took the table for themselves. One snapped his fingers for service, and his father rushed over to wait on them.

How long was Barn-acle planning to stay in Millbrook? When would he leave? Surely, no one as high and mighty and important as him would need to stay more than a couple of days on his way to Edilann.

Camilla placed a folded letter and a bracelet in front of Barnaby and scurried away. Gilberd watched as the man unfolded the letter, but with each passing second, his frown deepened, and rage spilled across his features.

Barnaby swore and lashed out at a glass of water on the table. The glass flew through the air and shattered on the floor. And then he strode toward the kitchen with a look of pure malice on his face. Gilberd barely managed to get there first, grabbed Mirabelle by the wrist, shoved her into the pantry, and shut the door when Barnaby stormed into the kitchen.

"You!" he shouted, pointing a finger at him. His face was red and blotchy from anger, lips curled in a snarl. "You are poisoning Mirabelle's mind. Stay away from her!" He spat on the floor. "Do you honestly think a tavern boy is good enough to take her as his bride? You are just a dumb, uneducated chump with no future other than waiting tables. She is beautiful and should be paraded before the king on a lord's arm." His voice slurred with drunkenness as he pointed to his chest. "You were born a nobody spill-wiper, and you will die a nobody spill-wiper."

For once, the anger fled Gilberd's body and was replaced by numbness. Words never usually hurt. But he was right. Mirabelle deserved better.

On his way out of the kitchen, Barnaby grabbed a glass from the counter and shattered it on the ground. Small shards skittered across the floor and then lay still.

Silence.

46

Gilberd felt his family's eyes on him, but all he could do was stare at the glass at his feet. He blinked slowly, heavily. And finally crouched to pick up the broken pieces. He wasn't sure what to feel. Embarrassment? Shame? Heartache?

But all he felt was numb.

Jeremy spoke first. "You are none of those things," he said softly.

And then his mother laid a gentle hand on his shoulder. "We regret not sending you to school. If we could have afforded it, we would have."

They had sent Jeremy to school to get an education. And then after the economy crashed, Gilberd never got an opportunity when he'd stayed to help his parents recover. He tried not to envy his older brother. But it was difficult. First, Jeremy had gotten a quality education. Then, he'd run off with his bride and followed his career dreams.

"It's fine," he murmured, throwing the broken shards of glass into the garbage pail.

A light hand touched his elbow, and he turned slightly to find Mirabelle gazing up at him, a mixture of fear and defiance in her eyes. "I think I am ready to go home. Will you still walk with me?"

After a moment's hesitation, he nodded. But as they exited the inn through the back door and walked side by side, his hands stuffed in his pockets, he didn't speak. There was nothing to say. Not anymore.

The moon lit their path, and a gentle summer breeze ruffed his hair and cooled the heat in his face. He stared at the dirt road and the rocks crunching beneath his boots. The night smelled of grass, hay, and hearth smoke. Yet, he couldn't appreciate it when he felt numb. Numb thoughts. Numb heart. Numb everything.

"You shoved me inside a closet again," Mirabelle commented suddenly, casting a sly, teasing grin at him.

He kicked a rock and watched it skitter across the road and into a pile of weeds. "It was a pantry. And for the record, I have never shoved you into a pantry before."

"There is a first for everything, I suppose."

He grunted noncommittally and kicked another rock. He knew what he needed to say next, but pure, absolute heartbreak squeezed his chest, cracking through his numb ribs. There was no future for them. He was just a dumb, nobody, spill-wiper boy. Marrying the lovely lady at his side had only been a distant dream. Always out of reach. Never attainable. "Listen, Mirabelle." He absently fiddled with his sleeve. "I should never have—"

"Will you go to the creek with me?"

Moisture burned his eyes and blurred his vision, and he kept his gaze on the ground to hide the emotion welling inside his chest. More than anything, he wanted to. But...

"I'll be too busy tomorrow and the rest of the week. And besides—"

"Tonight. I want to go tonight."

His chest felt heavy as if a sack of flour rested on his lungs. Barnaby's words continued to slice him, each stroke cutting through another layer of the numbness until he began to ache. "No. Another time."

When he took another step forward, he halted and breathed in sharply when Mirabelle slipped her hand into his. She didn't simply hold it but threaded each of her fingers through his. The intent was clear. But he couldn't understand her reasoning.

For a long moment, he stared down at their intertwined fingers. Her bandaged hands were small but soft. They were gentle yet gripped him with a sturdiness that spoke of her resilience on the ranch.

His heart thundered so loudly in his ears that he almost missed her next sentence.

"I really would like to go with you," she said quietly, gazing at him with what looked to be adoration, but he didn't dare hope.

A shuddering breath escaped his lips. "I'm no good for you. I can never introduce you to the king, the queen, the prince, or anyone of noble birth, really. I can't give you beautiful dresses and expensive jewelry."

"I never said I wanted those things."

Maybe not, but... "But you *did* say you wanted nothing to do with me, and you never wanted to go anywhere with me."

She squeezed his hand. "I changed my mind."

"Why?"

"Because there is more to you than I realized."

He knew he should drop her hand. But he couldn't bring himself to part from the warmth of her fingers or the soft skin of her hands. "And Barnaby helped you realize this?" he asked sarcastically, recalling his harsh but true words.

When she stepped closer, his heart squeezed in tandem. Even in the darkness, she had the most beautiful eyes framed by long, dark lashes. "The first thing you did when Barnaby came storming in was hide me. Protect me. Looking after others is second nature to you. You look after me. You help take care of your family. You watch out for those orphan boys."

"I only did what was right. That's all."

He grimaced when he realized just how much Barnaby's words had cut his soul. Tonight, his confidence was shattered. He'd tried for so long to become a good man that his mother would be proud of. But his lack of education truly made him doubt himself.

Surprise flashed across his face when she pulled him by the hand in the direction of the creek, and like a love-struck fool, he allowed it.

"Let's just leave it all behind," she said, smiling at him. "I don't know about you, but I've had a rough day. I could use a little bit of quiet."

"Quiet is not the word my mother would use to describe me," he chuckled. And why was he still following her? He should stop this.

But he couldn't. Because he adored this woman.

"You're right," she laughed, and he found himself smiling like an idiot at the sweetness of the sound. "I can easily pick you out of a crowd. You're tall *and* loud."

"Oh? I didn't realize you kept an eye out for me."

Her eyes shone with a mischievous glint. "Only sometimes."

A permanent grin lay across his face as he allowed her to take the lead. The rocky road transitioned into a dirt path shadowed by trees and bushes. The air dropped several degrees as they neared the creek. Trickling water slowly became louder until they stood several feet away from the river. Frogs croaked. Crickets chirped. A gentle breeze whispered through the trees.

Quiet.

Comforting.

The water traveled slowly down the riverbed, approximately waist deep, at least for him, judging by the water marks on the boulders at the edge of the creek.

Mirabelle released his hand and kicked off her shoes before settling down on a boulder, feet in the water. He joined her, pulling each boot and sock off and tossing them aside, followed by rolling up his pant legs to his knees. The frigid water felt refreshing against his submerged feet and ankles. Especially after a long, hard night of working at the inn.

He leaned back on his hands, closed his eyes, and released a sigh. It felt like such a long time since he'd found a spare minute to relax.

"Barnaby had no right to say any of those things."

And then his muscles tensed, all relaxation gone from his body the moment she uttered that name. He shifted his weight from his hands and rested his elbows on his knees while he stared at the languid water.

"He's not wrong. I am a poor, uneducated chump who will die a spill-wiper. Not all people get to play lords and nobles."

"Yet, he is spoiled, entitled, and unkind."

He puzzled over why she was courting the man in the first place. She'd expressed her lack of interest in marrying him, but...

For several moments, he debated how much he should tell her about Barnaby. Women seemed to be near oblivious to his faults, instead seeing the title, the money, and the good looks. Not what lay beneath it.

"Just…" He turned slightly to find her watching him, arms wrapped around one knee while her other foot soaked in the water. "Be careful with that man."

Her eyebrows furrowed together. "What do you mean?"

It was none of his business to wedge his foot into her courting life, no matter how much he wanted to insert himself. His father might get angry with him if he spread the information around, but perhaps she needed to know. "He has a lot of…female company…in his room at the inn. You deserve better than to be treated like that, with more than one woman in his life."

Disgust contorted her expression. She clearly hadn't known about Barnaby's intimate exploits. "No, Gilberd. You misunderstand. I ended things with him. That's likely why he was so angry today and said those hurtful things to you in the first place. I should never have started things with him to begin with."

"Oh." He released a long, slow breath, not knowing what, exactly, to do with the information. "But I thought your parents were putting pressure on you to marry."

"They are." Her somber gaze turned to the river. And when her chin trembled, his heart broke for her. He hovered his hand over her back, waiting, uncertain. He touched her lightly, and when she didn't protest, but rather leaned into the touch, he proceeded to wrap an arm around her.

She turned her face into his shoulder, seeking his comfort. This time, she didn't cry, as if she'd released all her pent-up tears earlier in the night. "My father doesn't have much time left." A long pause, and then her words escaped as a dry rasp. "I'm scared, Gilberd. What will I do?"

Absently, he circled his thumb on her arm, eyebrows furrowed. "Has your mother made funeral arrangements?"

"Yes, but nothing more. She's so used to Papa making all the decisions, I don't think she knows where to start when it comes to the ranch. She'd rather bury the issues and pretend like they don't exist."

"So you feel alone."

Mirabelle nodded and sighed the most exhausted sigh he'd ever heard. "My mother thinks that if I marry, a man can take care of my father's business without a hitch, and we needn't worry about things. I don't know if I can make that sacrifice."

"Marriage?"

"Marrying someone like Barnaby."

His thumb now made circles on her shoulder as he gazed into the darkness of the trees, deep in thought. Heat spiked in his blood when her head rested more fully against his shoulder, and he reminded himself to breathe when his lungs started to ache. He wanted to marry her, but asking now, when he hadn't courted her and she was truly vulnerable in that moment, would be a terrible idea.

However, he could still offer help.

"You're not alone." He dared to rest his chin on top of her head. The foreignness of holding her close sent a ball of tumbling nerves rolling down the hill of his stomach. He liked the way her floral scent teased his nostrils. He loved how they fit together, as if he could shield her entire body with his. He enjoyed the feeling of rightness, as if their souls had waited ages to touch. "I will help you however I can, and I know my mother is always there for you, as well as other townsfolk."

Slowly, she lifted her head until she stared into his eyes. The distrust in her expression tightened his gut with discomfort. "I remember the time when you said you would help me lift the water bucket out of the well. You dumped it over my head instead."

He squeezed his eyes shut and released a huff of frustration. At his younger self. At her flawless memory. At his stupidity. Why had he been so stupid back then? "I remember as well." He sighed again. "You'd been ignoring me for weeks. I took drastic measures to get your attention."

She lifted an eyebrow. "And you thought drenching me was the best way to accomplish that?"

"I know. I'm dumb." He squeezed her hand. "But I meant what I said. You're not alone."

The croaking frogs seemed to grow louder in the silence as she simply stared at him, but finally, she stood. Her sudden lack of heat against his side felt like a snip of thread. The moment was over. His chance was gone. But perhaps it was for the best.

An ache pushed against the inside of his ribcage at the thought.

"I can barely sit upright, I'm so tired," she said, starting back toward the path. "You don't need to walk me the rest of the way."

"Yes, I do." He awkwardly hopped after her as he tried to pull his socks and shoes back on in his haste to follow. "A woman should never walk alone at night."

"I've lived here almost my whole life, Gil."

A bright smile stretched across his face at his nickname on her lips. She'd never called him anything but Gilberd. And a few choice, nasty names. He'd deserved those. "So have I, Mira."

She paused in her step and glanced at him, but then her mouth twitched the slightest bit before she continued onward. She liked it! She liked his nickname for her.

They spoke no more words until they reached her home, and surprisingly, Mrs. Waters sat outside on the porch swing as if waiting for Mirabelle's return. The woman paused her knitting to smile at him.

"Good evening, Gilberd."

"Mrs. Waters. How are you?"

"Better now that my daughter is home. She knows I hate it when she disappears when it's dark."

He raised an eyebrow and Mirabelle, but she shuffled quickly toward the house. "Goodnight."

"Tomorrow!" he called after her, and she paused with her hand on the door to glance over her shoulder at him. "I expect you to have a list ready in the morning."

Without another word, he started back down the path. But when he reached home, he paused when he found Jeremy waiting for him in the back, arms crossed and a worried frown on his face. "We need to talk," his brother said, leaning a shoulder against the wall.

All the joy from his time with Mirabelle dissolved like sugar in hot tea. He remembered the last time Jeremy had used those words. Ten years ago. Right before he left home.

He glanced toward the window, watching his parents and sister-in-law cleaning up after supper inside. At the moment, he'd rather be scrubbing floors than facing his brother. "Surely, it can wait."

"Not really, no." Jeremy uncrossed his arms, and internally, Gilberd braced himself. "We wanted to tell you for months now, but we were waiting for the right opportunity. Tonight has proven I need to tell you now."

To avoid his brother's stare, Gilberd glanced up at the moon overhead and then turned to watch a couple of cup-shot men laugh and stumble down the road. Mr. Galloway's pig also wandered down the street in search of a late-night snack. How often did that ridiculous pig escape? Too much, he decided.

Jeremy sighed and finally gripped his arms to force him to look into his eyes. "You've given me ten years, Gilberd. Ten years to find myself. To find a wife. To start a family. I want to give you the same. We are moving back to Millbrook in autumn."

Shock coursed through him. Small, at first. And then it flooded through his mind, freezing his thoughts and muddling his brain. "What?" he croaked. "How? Why?"

Slowly, Jeremy nodded. "I found a new job here. Camilla will help at the inn. The children will be able to grow up in Millbrook. We bought a house, but we're currently waiting to be able to move in, as well as for our belongings to arrive across the sea."

He shook his head, trying to process his brother's words. "Why would you do this?"

"Because," Jeremy squeezed his arms, "you did it for me. Now you can do what you've always wanted. Go join the army. Serve the king."

The world spun suddenly in his shock, and he lowered himself onto a nearby bench to give his mind time to catch up. For all his life, he'd wanted to become a soldier. To train with the sword. To fight. To protect. He'd wanted nothing more.

But now?

Finally, he met Jeremy's eye. "I can't," he croaked. "I'll lose Mirabelle."

Though, he didn't even have her, and he began to suspect he never would. But unless she was completely off the market, he couldn't afford to leave.

The thought punched a hole in his gut. If he stayed in Millbrook, he would always be a spill-wiper boy. Never making a living for himself. Never doing something he truly loved. Jeremy was giving him an opportunity he might never get again.

Jeremy pulled a crinkled piece of parchment out of his pocket and smoothed it before handing it to him. To his own embarrassment, it took far too long to sound out the words in his head. He'd never had much practice with reading.

The king wants YOU!
If you want to learn how to fight with a sword,
then join the king's army.
Recruitment starts on the first day of the Mother Star.

Gilberd swallowed his shock and lifted his head from the parchment. "Recruitment starts in two weeks." That wasn't enough time to make Mirabelle fall madly in love with him. Not that he had much of a chance anyway.

"You would have to leave in a week and a half if you want to make it in time. Maybe sooner." Jeremy patted his back. "Something to think about."

He stared at his brother and then glanced down at the parchment in his hands. Beautiful brown hair, lively eyes, and a radiant smile came to mind. Mirabelle's laughter echoed in his head, and he couldn't help but imagine what a life with her might look like. Perhaps he could take over the ranch for her. When he came in after a long day of work in the hot sun, she would greet him with a kiss, and they would sit down to supper together. Perhaps have a few children of their own.

He wanted it so badly.

If he left, he risked losing his chance.

With a heavy heart, he handed the recruitment flier back to Jeremy and shook his head. "I can't."

And then he slipped inside the kitchen and got to work, more silent than ever. Giving up his dream broke his heart in two. But he suspected losing Mirabelle might shatter it altogether.

T he rooster crowed.

The stinky, rotten, horrible rooster!

Mirabelle groaned into her pillow and covered her ears to block out the approach of another dawn. The first rays of the day broke through the window and scratched her like a cat demanding milk straight from the utter.

She groaned again. Her head ached from crying so much last night. Her feet and hands burned with blisters all along her toes and fingers. Dread sliced through her when she thought of the milking and the weeding and the shoveling and the lifting. All her life, she'd always wanted a brother or two. But she wanted one now more than ever to share the heavy workload.

Once her father died, perhaps she could sell the cattle. But then what? What kind of living could she create for herself that would give her the means to support herself and her mother?

She pinched the bridge of her nose to ward off the ache festering between her eyes, but the moment she released the pillow, the rooster's crow grated against her mind. Had it been a mistake to dismiss Barnaby as a suitor?

Disgust pinched her mouth as she thought of what Gilberd had said about Barnaby's intimate pursuits. She refused to share a husband. No matter how comfortable he might make her life.

Someone knocked on the door of her bedroom, and she bolted upright in her bed. Moments later, her mother walked in. Panic consumed her at seeing her mother so early in the day, and she slipped off the bed and winced when the action pained her feet.

"Papa?" she asked.

"Sleeping," her mother answered, but then a slow, knowing smile pulled on her lips. "You never told me we'd have visitors. Otherwise, I would have had muffins waiting for those strapping young men."

"Strapping? Young men?" Mirabelle rubbed the sleep from her eyes and yawned now that her worry over Papa's health abated. "Who are you talking about?"

"That young man of yours brought some friends."

Her eyebrows furrowed in confusion. At least until someone's laughter outside brought her attention to the window. Loud laughter. Familiar laughter.

Her eyes snapped open wide, and she threw open the shutters to peer outside. Ice cold dread dumped a bucket of water over her head. "The Frightful Five!" she gasped in horror. Gilberd and his four rowdy, obnoxious friends were outside. Two pulled weeds. Another carried two empty pails. And Gilberd and one friend stood in the apple tree, pruning branches.

Each looked up from their task after her gasp, and smiles spread across each face.

"Mornin', Belle!" Sam called out to her with a wave, hand covered in a leather glove.

"Nice to see you again, M." Clark greeted her with a raise of his bucket. "Haven't seen you in a long while."

Hugh, the quieter one, simply nodded his head and returned to his weeding. Jude leaned precariously out of the tree and pointed his shears at her, a teasing grin on his face.

"We couldn't pass up an opportunity to see what Gil's excitement was about," the man called across the yard. "He fancied you for *years*, you know! What a sap!" A chorus of laughter followed. "Never seen someone so dejected for the longest time when you left Millbrook."

"Shut it," Gilberd growled as he shoved his friend, who might have fallen out of the tree if he hadn't tightly gripped a branch.

Mirabelle's cheeks flamed with heat as she met Gilberd's gaze from her place at the window. He'd fancied her for years? Of course, he'd mentioned he'd thought her cute. But actually fancied? For so long?

"What?" Jude protested, now pointing his shears at Gilberd. "Everyone knows it's true." He laughed, a glint in his eye as he called up to her again. "We've all fancied you at one time or another. Gilberd's fancy just never faded."

"Why, I'm gonna…" A tousle in the tree knocked several apples off the branches, followed by a spray of leaves. Despite herself, she giggled. Growing up, she'd hated all five of those boys, Gilberd the most. But they had all showed up to help her at the ranch? And so early in the morning?

Fire burned within her heart as she spotted Gilberd once more in the fray of leaves. A fondness. An overbearing warmth. Within the past couple of weeks, something had changed between them. A lot, perhaps. She'd gone from hating the man to...to...

She leaned against the window frame and smiled, absently running her hair through her fingers. She liked him quite a bit.

But then the heat transitioned into icy mortification when she realized she still wore her nightgown. She snapped the shutters closed and hurried to her wardrobe, snatched a dress, and changed into it.

"In a hurry to see your man?" her mother teased.

Mirabelle frowned as she tied her apron over her dress and began braiding her hair into a crown around her head. "He's not my man."

"The blossoming of new love on your face says otherwise."

She turned away when the heat became unbearable and focused on pinning her hair to her head. "There is nothing between us. Besides, I don't know how I feel about him."

Mama stole the last pin from her fingers and finished the braided ensemble with tremoring hands. "Your grandmother told me that the quickest way to sort through feelings is to kiss the man."

Nervousness turned her stomach as she gazed back at her mother through the mirror. "Not Gilberd."

"Who else would I be talking about?"

"I can't just," she glanced back and forth across the room and lowered her voice to a whisper, "kiss him."

"Why not?"

She slipped her boots on, if only to avoid getting teased by the boys for wandering around barefoot. Not liking the serious direction of the conversation, she teased back, "Because he's too tall for me to reach."

Her mother simply smiled and shook her head, and before the conversation could continue, she rushed into the hallway and paused before the front door. She smoothed her skirts, her hair, and then gently opened the door, willing her heart to reflect her outer calm.

It refused to obey.

Instead, it beat rather quickly with a strong, pounding tempo.

Gilberd's laughter drew her attention across the graveled yard toward the apple tree. From where he stood in the tree, he threw a rotten apple, and it splattered across Jude's chest. Jude attempted to retaliate with his own, but Gilberd ducked, and it missed.

She laughed at his playfulness. But the moment he turned his head in her direction, Jude threw another apple, and it splattered against Gilberd's shoulder. He scowled at his friend and flicked the rotten mess from his clothing while Jude hooted with laughter. But then her heart shook and trembled with nervousness when he climbed down and started toward her, his previous scowl melting into a warm expression.

"I need to feed the cattle!" she blurted.

"Already done."

"Milking then."

"Clark is on it."

"Weeding?"

He shooed her away toward the porch. "Consider this your day off."

"What am I supposed to do then?"

A grin spread across his face as he stretched his arms over his head, drawing her gaze to the muscles tight against his sleeves. "Perhaps enjoy the view?"

Amusement mimicked his grin on her face, and she reached into her pocket and slapped a piece of paper against his chest. The hard muscles were solid against her palm, inciting a tumble of nerves through her stomach. "I made a list, just as you requested."

Then she inwardly cringed at her insensitivity. In the big city, plenty of people knew how to read. Her mother could read, which was how Mirabelle had learned. Her father could read very little, never having had the need or interest to learn. But what about Gilberd?

Therefore, she listed the tasks off on her fingers as well. "Move the hay from the wagon to the barn. Fix the porch railing." She wiggled a loose piece of wood as a demonstration. "Prune the tree, which you were already doing. There are also shingles missing on the roof. But I can do that."

"No," he said immediately. "You are not getting up there."

"That's a shame." She shrugged and turned away, but not before casting a coy glance at him. "I've heard roofs are great places to share stolen kisses."

"I mean…" He shrugged as well and returned her coy look. "I suppose the roof isn't *too* dangerous."

When he made to grab her hand, she laughed and lunged away. Although she enjoyed teasing him, her mother's words still prodded at her mind. What if she kissed Gilberd? How would he react? How would she react? Did she even want to?

But as he gazed at her with deep, soulful brown eyes, she realized that yes, she *did* want to kiss him. She wanted to kiss him. She wanted him to hold her like he had last night. She wanted to find out what could blossom between them.

"Keep in mind, Keats," she pushed him away with a finger to his chest and wrinkled her nose, "you smell like rotten fruit."

"Fair enough. But if you change your mind, you know where to find me."

She felt his gaze on her until she disappeared inside the house and into the kitchen. From the window, she had a good view of him as he returned to prune the rest of the branches. As she cracked eggs into a bowl and whipped them with a fork, she contemplated their relationship. How had they gone from enemies to flirting?

Mama joined her minutes later with a pail filled with milk and set it on the table. "Such good boys. I bet they all make their mothers proud."

Thinking of Mrs. Keats last night, Mirabelle smiled. "I'm sure they do."

The pan sizzled when she scooped the beaten eggs into it, stirring them until they scrambled. Along with the muffins her mother started making, it was enough to feed six hungry men. She finished the meal off with seasoned apples and glasses of milk.

"Has Papa eaten yet?" she asked, but her mother shook her head. "He had a bad night and has been sleeping all morning."

They shared a look of heartache and sympathy. She wished he didn't have to suffer anymore, but at the same time, she was terrified of losing him.

Quietly, she made another plate and entered her father's room, surprised to find him sitting upright on his own. His face was pale, eyes dark from lack of sleep, hair greasy and matted. "I took it out yesterday," he mumbled. "They didn't want it."

"Who didn't want it?" She sat in the chair beside the bed.

"They." Frustration contorted his expression as he gestured to the wall. So, this was what her mother had meant when she mentioned a bad night. The moments of clarity in his mind became rarer by the day. "They will take you instead. I've always been terrified they will take you!" He knocked a tankard of water off the bedside table, and it clattered on the ground. "It's not enough. It's not enough. It's not enough."

"Papa," she soothed, taking his rough, clammy hand. "I'm here. No one has taken me."

"But they will!" he sobbed. "I wish you were born ugly. They will take you."

He struck out at the plate in her hand, but before he made contact, someone reached over her shoulder and grabbed his wrist. Rather than encouraging more violent behavior, the shock of the grab seemed to put more clarity into her father's eyes.

"Sir," Gilberd said, the heat of him seeping into her shoulder, "you have a mighty fine horse in your barn."

"My horse…" Papa murmured and retracted his hand from Gilberd's grip. "Yes, the horse." He blinked several times and then returned Gilberd's gaze. "I got him near ten years ago at an auction. He's never failed me."

"I don't doubt it. I remember you used to ride him through town. I told myself that one day, I would own a horse as fine as the one Mr. Waters rode."

Papa smiled and sank into his pillows. "Those were the best days." He yawned. "The very best." And then he closed his eyes, his chest rising and falling slowly with sleep.

"Would it help if we opened a window for him?" Gilberd asked quietly behind her.

She shook her head, set the plate on the table, and turned in her chair to face him. The man's mere height made her have to crane her neck to look at him. "The hay and dust in the air make him cough until he coughs up blood." The words on her tongue halted, but then she said, "How did you do that?"

"Do what?" Without preamble, he stooped to pick up the tankard. Warmth filled her heart at the reflexive action, the goodness, the kindness.

"Calm him down so easily. When he gets in these moods, it's hard to pull him out of them."

His eyes glinted with amusement, now level with hers. "There are fewer things a man is prouder of than his horse. Another would be offspring, as well as house and land."

"How do you know?" She outwardly cringed at the insensitivity of her words. Again.

"I'm incredibly observant." He didn't seem to take offense to her comment.

Her heart tumbled in her chest as she gazed into his eyes, face only inches from hers. Her mother's words echoed in her mind. *The quickest way to sort through feelings is to kiss the man.*

With a pounding pulse in her ears, she murmured his name and placed her hand on his broad shoulder. He stiffened against her, but otherwise remained still. In a moment of bravery, she leaned toward him. A part of her expected him to turn away in rejection. But instead, he also leaned toward her.

The sweet scent of apple on his breath brushed her skin. The entire core of her being burned with anticipation. But just as their noses brushed, followed by a flurry of butterflies in her stomach, someone tapped on the doorframe.

"Breakfast is ready!"

They jumped apart, only to find Jude standing in the doorway. In her fluster, she smoothed down her skirts and busied herself by tucking the sheets around her father.

Avoiding meeting Gilberd's gaze, she scurried past him and ducked out of the room.

"You idiot," Gilberd growled quietly, followed by a yelp from Jude. "You get to muck out the stalls now."

Heat spread across her face, and she avoided the stares of the other three boys as well from where they sat around the kitchen table.

"Did he eat?" Mama asked. But when she shook her head, her mother sighed as she took the muffins out of the tin and placed them on a plate. Her hands shook, and her gaunt frame told Mirabelle she likely hadn't eaten much lately either.

Silently, she squeezed her mother's hand. *It will all be fine,* she wanted to say. But they both knew those words would be a lie. So, she said nothing.

She took the plate from her mother, face still hot as she set it on the table. She jumped, startled when the five of them attacked the muffins as if they were all dying of hunger, and the only way to eat was to outpace the others. Within seconds, the plate was empty.

"Well," Mirabelle laughed, wiping her hands together and placing her fists on her hips. "I had no idea men had such ravenous appetites."

Clark groaned, mouth full. "These are so good, Mrs. Waters."

Mama waved his compliment away with a hand, and the others echoed with more full mouths and grunts of satisfaction. It was almost comical the way five grown men huddled at the table, hardly able to fit within the small dining area. She made the mistake of glancing at Gilberd, watching as a grin spread across his face.

The roof? he mouthed, wiggling his eyebrows.

She simply rolled her eyes and turned her back to him, hiding the soft smile growing on her own lips.

C rinkle.

Gilberd frowned as he glanced down at the paper he stepped on, and his frown only deepened as he stooped to pick up the familiar flier lying at the base of his bedroom door.

The king wants YOU!

Jeremy walked down the hallway at that moment, yawning. Or at least feigning a yawn. "Did I drop that?" he asked innocently, rubbing sleep from his eyes, but Gilberd noticed him trying to hide a grin beneath his hands.

"I told you already," he growled as he stuffed the flier into his pocket to get rid of later. "I don't want it."

"Liar. You *do* want it. You are just too stubborn to admit it."

Their voices lowered when they stepped foot into the guest hallway. A female giggle muffled from within Barnaby's room made him pause. Dread spiked in his blood, but it calmed a fraction when the woman giggled again. It was not Mirabelle. Of course, it wasn't. But some irrational part of him feared Barnaby would get his way in the end.

Calm down, he told himself, continuing on his way toward the kitchen with his brother at his heels. *Mirabelle is smarter than that.*

Deflecting Jeremy's question, he asked, "How long is Barnaby staying in Millbrook?"

His brother shrugged. "Until his business here is concluded, I assume."

"What does he do again?"

"Offers loans for new businesses and invests in initial startup costs." They entered the kitchen, and Jeremy's voice lowered even further. "I heard a rumor that he's tripled his wealth since the economy crashed."

"I sure hope not." He grabbed a pair of work gloves hanging beside the door and slipped on his sturdy boots. "What about the businesses? How are they profiting?"

A shrug. "I'd assume they are slowly able to pay off the loans."

Gilberd frowned, pausing in the doorway leading outside. When he noticed their mother walking past the kitchen with arms full of dirty sheets, he spoke quietly. "Our parents can't even pay *me* for the work I do here. And we're doing better than most."

In fact, he'd bartered service after service until he'd eventually been able to purchase his sword. Before then, he and Jeremy had carved sticks to use for swordplay.

A grimace contorted Jeremy's expression. "Now I feel even guiltier for leaving Edilann. You don't earn a wage?"

"I earn it through good food and a place to stay." What more could he say? Sure, he would love to earn his own wage to pay for his own home and support his own wife and children someday. But...

The flier in his pocket seemed to grow hotter and hotter, demanding attention.

He ignored the burn but couldn't ignore the heartache of longing. He had nothing to offer Mirabelle. Nothing. His only hope of a future with her was if she and her mother came to live at the inn after her father passed, or if he took over the ranch through marriage.

If she would have him, that was.

"Gil, I'm terribly sorr—"

"Save it," he grumbled. "Give it a couple more years, and the economy will flourish again."

Thankfully, his brother dropped the subject but teasingly called after him on his way to the main road. "Off to Mirabelle's?"

With a grin, he waved his limp gloves at Jeremy. "Hay isn't going to lift itself!"

Giddiness climbed through his chest at the thought of seeing her again. She was like the first rays of morning breaking over the horizon. Full of light, life, hope, and laughter.

He breathed in the crisp, fresh air of a summer morning. He nodded at passing travelers and other townsfolk riding a horse or driving a wagon. He stopped to pet a stray dog waddling down the road. The atmosphere felt familiar. Peaceful. Hopeful and promising.

"Out of my way!" someone shouted behind him, and like a few others on the road, he jumped to the side and hugged the edge of the ditch.

Very briefly, he recognized the rider as Barnaby as the man thundered by atop his horse. Too late to dodge, Barnaby spit at him. It was so sudden, so jarring, that he stumbled backward and nearly tripped into the ditch.

He angrily wiped the spittle from his face.

"You good for nothing, whiner baby, son of a scat!" he shouted. But then his eyes flashed open, and dread pounded in his temple as he watched the dust settle in the man's wake. Barnaby wasn't headed out of town. He was headed to Mirabelle's ranch.

He swore.

And then he started running.

M irabelle hummed a joyful tune at the edge of the creek, dunking each dirtied garment into the water and scrubbing with lye soap. Laundry was one of her least favorite chores, but today she found it enjoyable and relaxing. Especially knowing she wouldn't have to do much of the difficult chores because Gilberd promised to help.

At the thought of him, her heart stirred in a frenzied warmth, and a silly smile spread across her face and stayed. She continued to scrub Papa's shirt with the soap, humming in tune with each movement.

Time passed too slowly. But when she heard boots crunch against rocks behind her, followed by a snapping stick, her stomach fluttered with excitement.

Don't let him know how much you've looked forward to seeing him, she told herself sternly in her head.

But when she turned to greet Gilberd, she froze. Dread widened her eyes and rushed over her like an icy bath. Dread and horror and sick, sick discomfort.

Barnaby scowled at her from where he stood on the path leading back to the house. His horse remained several steps behind him, unknowingly blocking the way of escape.

"I did not appreciate the letter you wrote me," he started with arms crossed. "We are not done unless *I* say we're done. And I'm not through with you."

When he uncrossed his arms and stalked toward her, she abandoned the shirt at the edge of the creek and attempted to dart past him. He blocked her path. True, inescapable fear squeezed her chest. Although Barnaby wasn't as tall or as large as Gilberd, he was still bigger and stronger than her.

"Leave me alone!" she shouted in his face, trying not to cower when his expression contorted in a snarl.

"You don't understand how this works. We will marry in Edilann in one month's time. End of discussion."

Her voice trembled. "No."

"You will comply," he seethed inches from her face. "I *own* you."

She gasped at the ludicrous statement and shoved his chest, but he didn't budge. "Leave. Now." But her words seemed to fly over his head.

"I tried to do this the easy way, Mirabelle, by romancing you and giving you compliments and nice gifts. I tried to give you a choice. But now you don't get a choice."

Fear trembled in her heart, and she backed up farther until her shoulder blades scraped against the nearby tree. "Why?" she rasped. "How could you possibly benefit from marrying someone of my station?"

Many other eligible candidates existed with better fortunes and family ties.

Quicker than a striking snake, Barnaby grabbed a hold of her chin and tipped her head up. A cruelty she hadn't noticed before lived in his eyes. A determination to get what he wanted, no matter the cost. "You truly do not understand how alluring you are, do you?" She flinched away when he trailed a finger down her throat. "Do you know how many noblemen would love to have a turn in bed with a strikingly beautiful woman? With you as my wife, do you understand how many favors the nobility could owe me?"

Mirabelle's face paled. Her stomach churned with sickening nausea. "You would pass me around the upper class?"

"Discreetly, of course. After I've had my own fun."

How could someone do something so horrid to another person?

Vines of horror strangled her lungs. Squeezing tighter, tighter, tighter until darkness flooded the edges of her vision. Her body swayed, and she tipped precariously to the side as she lost her balance and her footing. Barnaby reached out for her, but instead of grabbing her, he knocked her further off balance and she pitched to the side.

Splash!

The shock of frigid water engulfing her startled her consciousness back to the surface, only for panic to set in. The creek dragged her downstream, a flash of brown, green, and blue passing in a blur. Her lungs burned. She kicked and clawed to keep her head above the water, but the stream fought against her.

"What did you do?" she barely heard Gilberd's voice through the water rushing in her ears. "She can't swim!"

She opened her mouth to call out for him but instantly regretted it when water rushed in. She coughed and sputtered, her body spinning in the water until she faced backward instead of forward. Her head submerged, blinding her once again. A dip in the current slammed her against a wall of rocks. Pain coursed through her head and shoulder, and a second cloud of darkness shrouded her vision.

She blacked out for several moments until another wave of panic set in. White water crashed over her head, pushing her farther into the river. And just when her body threatened to give out, a strong arm wrapped around her waist and hauled her to the surface.

Air entered her lungs in gasps, choking, and splutters. Dark spots floated in her vision in tune with the spinning and buzzing in her head. She clung to her rescuer's shoulders, and when Gilberd's comforting voice murmured in her ear, she held tighter.

Her head still spun as he heaved her out of the stream, gently laying her onto a bank of soft grass. Each breath she took burned her lungs, and she squeezed her eyes shut when the throbbing in her temple pained her too much.

"Mira," Gilberd said in a frantic voice, shaking her shoulders. "Mira, answer me."

A groan escaped her mouth moments before she turned onto her side and vomited into the grass. Everything hurt. Her muscles. Her head. Her shoulder. Her lungs.

"You're bleeding."

Mirabelle cracked her eyes open just enough to find him pulling a sopping wet shirt over his head and holding it against her temple. Pain burned at the contact, and she groaned again.

Gilberd's worried eyes settled on her, damp hair clinging to his forehead. Despite the fire in her lungs and pounding in her head, she couldn't help but appreciate the deep brown of his eyes, his masculine jaw, and the reddish-brown beard on his face. Her gaze dipped to his bare chest, and she smiled exhaustedly.

"This is the second time you've been shirtless in my presence," she croaked.

"That's because I enjoy how you can't help but look," he teased back, but concern still rippled across his pained expression. "This is a lot of blood. I need to take you to the doctor in town."

Salty tears leaked from the corners of her eyes, mingling with the water dripping from her face. "I can't. There is so much work to do here. And…and…" She winced. "I don't have money to pay."

"I'll barter services. I'll give my time." He ran a hand over her hair and gently cupped her cheek, gazing at her with a tortured yet tender expression. "I need you to be all right."

The green of the leaves in the canopy above blended when her world continued to spin. "I don't want to go to the doctor. I just want to lie down."

"Stubborn woman," he breathed, but he still gripped her hand gently. "I'll take you to my mother then."

She nodded but winced. "Not without your shirt, though. People will get the wrong idea." She meant it as a jest. However, she could barely manage a laugh.

He chuckled and scooped her up, one arm behind her back and the other beneath her legs while she held the sopping shirt to her head. He carried her at a rapid pace toward the road, moving smoothly as if afraid to jostle her. "In all honest truth, there are worse ideas for people to get."

Instead of holding in tears of pain, she blinked back tears of emotion. "Gil," she whispered, which turned his attention from the path ahead to her. She placed her free hand behind his neck and pulled him closer until their lips met in the sweetest, gentlest kiss.

Her heart fluttered within her ribcage. Her stomach tied in knots. For a moment, all of the pain fled her body, replaced by unbridled relief at how right it felt to be held by him, to receive his kiss.

Soft, damp hair brushed against her skin as she tangled her fingers through his hair. With what little strength she had, she pulled herself tighter against him. A fever of emotion ran through her body. Relief. Happiness. Desire.

Slowly, her hand moved from his hair, down his neck, and over his chest. The strong muscles connected with her fingertips, but the touch seemed to fluster Gilberd. He tripped over a rock on the road, his shout of surprise muffled by her lips, the contact promptly broken. He barely seemed able to catch himself.

"Ah!" he gasped, righting his balance before scolding her teasingly. "No walking and kissing. You are living on the edge today."

A weak laugh rolled off her tongue, but she instantly regretted it when her skull continued to pound relentlessly. She groaned and leaned more heavily against Gilberd's shoulder. Pain battered her skull, and the bright light of morning suddenly became too much to bear.

"Mirabelle!" Barnaby's voice called after them. She squeezed her eyes shut in an attempt to block out the sound. Gilberd increased his pace. "Wait!"

Although she continued to keep her eyes shut, she felt Gilberd's voice reverberate in his chest against his ear, fury raging in every syllable. "If I see your lousy arse around Mirabelle again, I will smash your face in, and then I will break all your fingers. Understand?"

"I—"

"Not a word."

Thankfully, Barnaby didn't speak again as if afraid Gilberd would make good on his threat.

Exhaustion in body and soul weighed her down, pulling her deeper into the darkness. At least until Gilberd softly patted her cheek. "Don't fall asleep. We're almost there."

The air transitioned from cool to warm with a hint of freshly baked bread. Several gasps startled her in her exhaustion, but when she tried to open her eyes, the light seared her once again. Too bright.

"Ma," Gilberd said, voice calm and controlled despite his tight, anxious grip on her. "She fell in the creek. Hit her head on a rock. Can you help?"

Someone pulled the wet shirt out of her hand and inhaled sharply before it was replaced by a dry cloth, several loose threads brushing her cheek. "You poor dear," Mrs. Keats said, and she opened her eyes enough to find the woman searching her face for other injuries. Camilla stood just behind her.

"The rooms are full," she continued.

Gilberd started forward. "My room then."

He climbed the stairs with ease and entered a room at the back of a secluded hallway, the other two women following close behind. But when he tried to set her on the bed, she protested.

"I don't want to get it wet."

"I don't care about that."

"Gil."

Mrs. Keats interrupted. "Set her in the chair for now. Grab a drying cloth and a dress from my wardrobe. And don't come back in."

Now in a chair, she felt unsteady, even sitting. Her mind continued to spin, but less so now. The moment Gilberd left and closed the door behind him, Mrs. Keats lifted the cloth again and frowned.

"Head injuries tend to bleed a lot, but this likely isn't as terrible as it looks. Bear with me, Mirabelle. I am going to braid your hair around the wound to close the cut rather than use stitches. It will hurt less this way, and it's just as effective."

She winced, but otherwise gave no other indication of her discomfort when Mrs. Keats started braiding her hair meticulously, concentration on her brow. Shivers wracked her entire frame, her body finding it difficult to maintain warmth after the shock of almost drowning and the chill of the water. Her limbs felt heavy, too stiff and achy to move.

As Mrs. Keats braided her hair, Camilla began unbuttoning the back of Mirabelle's dress.

"G-G-Gill will come back i-i-in," she protested, teeth chattering.

"He won't," Camilla assured. "Though, I can't promise he won't be pacing a hole through the floors until he's allowed to see you."

Once again, she found herself under the administration of this incredible, kind family. "I-I-I apologize for being such a p-p-pain this week."

"You are not a pain." Mrs. Keats gently touched her hand. "You are a blessing."

"Wh-wh-what do you m-m-mean?"

The other two women shared a significant look. Mrs. Keats answered, attention once again focused on the task of tightly braiding the small portion of hair. "It's hard to watch my son despair over his own future. Or lack thereof. But he has been happier lately."

"Not because of m-m-me."

Instead of answering, she shrugged.

Camilla pulled Mirabelle's arms out of her sleeves, and she involuntarily hissed at the way the fabric rubbed on her injured shoulder. The skin was scraped and raw. Red and burning, tender to the touch. Despite the pain, she found reprieve with her wet clothing off, and her shivering slowly subsided after Camilla wrapped a blanket over her.

Mrs. Keats moved slower now as she wrapped her shoulder with a bandage. Camilla washed the blood from her hair with a wet cloth, the bowl quickly becoming red and murky.

"Gilberd said you fell into the creek?" Mrs. Keats' gentle movements lulled her closer to sleep. Her entire body felt worn and exhausted. It didn't help that Gilberd's scent leaked from the blanket around her, comforting and safe.

"Barnaby said something terrible to me. It made me sick and dizzy. I don't think he meant to push me into the creek when he tried to grab me."

Another significant look between the other two. "What did he tell you?"

Despite the chill in her bones, she flushed with heat. Embarrassment. Horror. Disgust. "I don't want to say."

A knock at the door froze her limbs over with ice once more, made worse when she heard Gilberd on the other side informing them he brought the requested items. But he didn't enter the room. Rather, when Camilla opened the door a crack, his hand appeared with the dry dress and cloth in tow, and then it disappeared after the door shut.

Together, Mrs. Keats and Camilla helped dry the rest of her off and dressed her. The sleeves were a bit too long, and she tripped on the hem of the dress on her way toward the bed. Several moments after her head met the pillow, her weary body succumbed to the relief of sleep.

Only for her to wake to the soft murmur of conversation and clinking dishes. She lifted her head, blinking back the light of dusk entering through the window. Pain crackled through her skull like lightning shooting through a gray sky, and she returned her head to rest. Thankfully, her body ached less, though her lungs still felt tender with each breath.

The comforting scent of Gilberd wafted off the pillow beneath her head. The more often she came across it, the more she liked it. Comforting. Thrilling. She inhaled deeply, taking in the scent. Memorizing it. Cherishing it.

"Did you just smell my pillow?"

Mirabelle shot into a sitting position but instantly regretted it when a fierce ache pounded in her temples. Gilberd stood at the foot of the bed, his arms crossed and a smirk on his mouth. Despite the pain, she denied it. "Of course not! I was just breathing. Heavily." And how long had he been standing there?

Irritating laughter escaped him and shook the very foundation of the room. She opened her mouth to tell him off, but her chest squeezed in surprise when he caught her chin with gentle fingers. He glanced back and forth between her eyes, and then turned her head to peer at the cut held together by a small, intricate braid.

A self-conscious wince puckered the skin around her eyes. Surely, there would be a scar left behind in the aftermath of the river scare. Barnaby would have found fault with it. Did Gilberd?

As if sensing the direction of her thoughts, he dropped her chin. "Two years ago, I fell off the roof and cut my cheek." He pointed to a silvery scar barely visible beneath a short layer of facial hair. "I grew out my beard to hide it while it healed. Ma kept saying the right kind of woman would find it attractive." He shrugged while grinning sheepishly. "I haven't shaved in a while. Likely because I haven't found that woman yet."

She found herself studying his face, wondering what he might look like without facial hair and a scar on his cheek. All she managed to conjure up was an image of a ruggedly handsome Gilberd.

"And my inevitable scar?"

"A token of your bravery facing the unforgiving waters of the creek. I find that very attractive."

Heat burned her face, only seeming to grow hotter when his characteristic smirk made an appearance right on time. To hide her fluster, she raised an eyebrow as high as possible before it protested against the strain on her tender scalp.

"The roof, Gil? That couldn't be why you refused to allow me to go up there."

He shrugged and ran a hand over his chin. "I'm not keen on heights. But I'd rather face them than risk your safety." Quickly, his eyes widened. "Oh!" He grabbed a plate filled with meat, steaming potatoes, and vibrant cooked carrots and set it on the bed beside her. "This is why I came up. I knocked first, but you were asleep. I didn't mean to stay to watch you *breathe heavily* against my pillow."

She grabbed the pillow in question and smacked him with it as hard as she could, but he only laughed and darted out of the way of her second attack.

Moving far too nimbly for someone his size, he slipped out the door, but not before calling over his shoulder. "All of your chores are done. Your mother knows where you are. You are welcome to stay the night."

"I'm not staying in here with you overnight."

"I wasn't planning on it." He smirked. "But if you insist…"

This time, she threw the pillow across the room, but it landed in a heap at his feet. His laughter was muffled by the door as he closed it. In all honesty, she had no desire to stay here, especially knowing that Barnaby might be sleeping several rooms away.

Even if this was Gilberd's bed.

A sigh left her lips as she ran a hand over the soft white sheets, her fingers grasping the fabric as confusion and indecision warred within her. What now? She'd kissed Gilberd. What came after?

The kiss played again in her mind. The beautiful, warming, heart-stopping kiss. Heat burned in her chest, seeming to grow hotter when she placed her hand over her erratic heart. Her mother had been right. The quickest way to figure out one's feelings for a man was to kiss him.

She was falling in love with Gilberd Keats.

And she wanted to see him again.

After consuming the meal as fast as she dared, she hesitantly peeked her head out of the room and into the secluded hallway. She steeled her nerves and took a single step, and then another, before tiptoeing across sturdy wooden floorboards, down a flight of stairs, and she easily found the kitchen, ducking inside to avoid attention from patrons in the dining room.

"Oh!" Mr. Keats said, surprise written on his face. The man was shorter than Gilberd and had gentler features. But she recognized his son in his eyes. They were the same color and contained much of the same intelligent scrutiny. "Good to see you awake. Gilberd is out back."

"I wasn't looking…" But the man disappeared before she managed to finish her sentence. Oh, who was she fooling? Yes, she was looking for Gilberd.

Both he and Jeremy entered through the back door, laughing as they each carried a bundle of wood into the kitchen to use for the stove. His eyes sparkled with amusement the moment he met her gaze. Nerves tumbled through her stomach as she realized she could easily imagine life with him. Smiles. Teasing. Laughter. Joy.

Love.

She wanted that. But she didn't know how to go about getting it.

A piece of parchment slipped out of Gilberd's pocket and fluttered onto the floor like the flitting wings of a bird. When he didn't seem to notice, she moved toward it and picked it up, reading the short message.

She blinked in surprise, holding it up for him to see after he deposited his bundle of wood beside the stove. "Are you going to the recruitment?" she asked.

"No." But the disappointment in his expression expressed volumes about that decision. She'd had no idea he was interested in becoming a soldier. The thought terrified her. But it also made her proud.

"Why not?"

Jeremy called across the room, "Because he's so afraid to lose you if he leaves!"

Gilberd curved his fingers, mimicking strangling. "I will wring your neck, Jer."

Yet, the truth of his fear shone in his eyes, in the pucker of his mouth. The absolute regret and devastation in his expression was subtle, but it was there. If he didn't leave within a few days, he might not make it in time. But what then? What would happen to their blossoming relationship? Her father would die, and he would miss it. Ownership of the ranch would be hefted onto her shoulders. He would miss that, too. How long would he be gone? How could they make this work? Would she have to move to Edilann where he would inevitably be stationed should he be recruited?

So many questions beat upon her mind, enough to cause the pounding in her temple to return. And with those questions came far too many emotions. Pride. Worry. Hope. Fear. Regret.

He couldn't stay for her. He had to know she would wait for him. But with their short acquaintance since her return to Millbrook, how could she possibly bring it up?

"Don't listen to my brother," Gilberd growled. "I don't want to go to recruitment. End of story."

Liar, her heart whispered.

"Well, I, for one, would like to go," she jested. "I would look great in a suit of armor."

The two brothers looked at her, then at each other, before bursting into laughter. She tried to feign a scowl, but it proved difficult when her words wiped his frown away.

An amused grin on his face, Gilberd approached and tenderly caressed her chin with his thumb. "I don't think they make a suit in your size, love."

Love...

Her feet floated on a cloud, her heart drifting alongside them in the gentlest of breezes on a warm, sunny afternoon. That settled it. She would go anywhere with this man. Even to Edilann.

"Gil," Mrs. Keats said behind them, and Mirabelle jumped and spun around to find the woman clearly trying to hold back a smile. "I have a few deliveries that need to go out tonight. Can you...?" She held out a basket, and Gilberd took it from her. Then, she carefully checked the wound on the side of Mirabelle's head. "It should be healed before you know it."

Mirabelle gently touched the small braid. "Thank you."

"Think nothing of it."

Gilberd gave her one last smile before ducking back out the door. She paused for a moment, wondering if she should stay. In the end, she ignored the ache in her body as she darted after him and fell into step beside him. Chickens squawked and waddled across the road. A pig sniffed on the grass growing at the base of a low stone wall outside someone's home, the owner tending to the vegetable garden out front.

Although nearly sunset, the sky above darkened with the promise of a summer storm. The smell of sweet rain lingered in the air she breathed, in the taste on her tongue.

"You should be resting," he scolded her.

"I rested all day."

Another long pause. "Camilla told me Barnaby said something to you. What did he say?"

Despite the calm way he spoke, thunder rolled across his face, a prelude to what was sure to follow in the sky later. He kept his gaze forward, though his white-knuckled grip around the handle of the basket spoke of his silent fury.

"I cannot speak of it," she croaked, lungs flaming once more with each word. "It's too vile to utter."

His nostrils flared, his expression seething. Words too deep and quiet for her to comprehend escaped his mouth like a string of muttered curses. Slowly, his knuckles became whiter than cattle bones.

The man's expression contorted with dark fury, and suddenly, he appeared scary and foreboding next to his height and brawn. Yet, she felt safer by his side than anywhere in the kingdom.

At the reminder, she stepped closer to him and looped her arm around his. The storm in his eyes calmed a fraction as he glanced down at her, and when she squeezed his bicep, the rage disappeared altogether as if forgotten.

He held her gaze long enough for her the tips of a thousand butterfly wings to brush against the inside of her ribcage.

"May I kiss you again?" he murmured, and those butterflies swarmed faster. Brighter. Hotter.

"No," she breathed.

His expression fell as if icy raindrops followed in the wake of his previous thunder. He became silent, his gaze on his feet and the rocks scattering with each step. But she didn't allow him to spiral farther as she slipped her hand down his arm and threaded her fingers through his.

Her next words escaped as a whisper. "Not where others can witness."

She heard his breath hitch, but before he spoke a single word, she glanced at their surroundings to make sure no one watched as she pulled him off the main road and into a thicket of pear trees in a small orchard.

The sweet fruit filled the air around them. Enticing. Beckoning. Yet hushed as if keeping a gratifying secret. Several bees buzzed above her head as she continued to lead Gilberd into the heart of the orchard until nothing surrounded them but dense leaves, ripe fruit, and the quiet stillness that came before a stormy night.

But when she turned to face Gilberd, a sudden nervousness shrouded her judgment, especially when he gazed at her with blazing eyes, missing no detail. His attention dropped from her eyes to her lips, and her heart responded with unbearable warmth.

Nerves shivered down her arms, but she forced them not to tremble when she lifted her hand and ran a finger over the scar hidden beneath his facial hair. "You know," she said quietly, afraid to disturb the growing flames sprouting from the ground between them, "I would like to see you clean-shaven. I think you would look rather handsome."

"Oh, really?" He leaned closer until the breath from his lips brushed her ear, sending a pleasant shiver down her spine.

"I will keep your words in mind tomorrow when you run in the opposite direction."

"I think you are mistaken in which direction I will be running."

The fire in his eyes smoldered brighter, visible passion growing in his expression that likely mimicked hers. Heat followed in the wake of his touch as he slipped an arm around her waist and pulled her flush against him. No inch of space remained between them.

"Mira," he murmured, her name on his tongue filling her with heady longing.

She stood on her toes and snaked her arms around his shoulders, their lips only a breath apart. To her delightful surprise, she'd been wrong. She *could* reach him. But not without him dipping his head first.

"What's so funny?" he asked, and until then, she hadn't realized she'd giggled.

"I wasn't sure I would be able to reach you." Her fingers played with the hair at the nape of his neck.

"You thought about kissing me before, have you?"

"Only a few times. I—"

His lips met hers, cutting off her next few words. She breathed in his scent. She allowed her hands to roam over his arms. Searching. Seeking. Exploring. Every fiber of her being thrummed alive, growing more insistent as he backed her against the nearest tree until she was most pleasantly pinned against the trunk. Trapped in the rapture of his touch. His kiss.

With gentle fingers that also held the strength of confidence, he lifted her arms above her head and pinned her hands against the tree, deepening the kiss. A sigh escaped her, followed by weakened legs that threatened to melt her in his embrace. In a single moment, he managed to wipe all doubt and hesitance from her mind.

If he asked for her hand, she would agree in a heartbeat.

She wanted this man. Forever.

The kiss ended all too soon, but the satisfaction of a mouth well-explored allowed her to savor the taste of his lips.

"I will wait for you," she whispered as she gazed back at him, chest rising and falling rapidly from both heated passion and nervous excitement. "If you want to become a soldier, I will wait for you."

For several long moments, he stared back at her, saying nothing. But the disbelief and uncertainty in his expression was plain to see. A silent battle raged in his eyes. Heat. Fire. Hope. But it was as if a blizzard put out the flames, and they glassed over with despondent ice.

He traced the curve of her jaw before tipping her chin up with a finger and bestowing a sweet, gentle kiss on her lips. "It's not the right time," he murmured. "I can't leave you now."

A pit formed in her stomach upon realizing what his words meant. Her father was dying. She and her mother would be left on their own with the funeral and figuring out what to do with the ranch. Yes, she needed him. She knew she did. But she hated coming between him and his dreams.

She couldn't.

No matter what it took, what it cost her, she would get him to Edilann. Even if she had to go behind his back to do it.

M irabelle strode toward the Keats' inn and residence with purpose in each stride. In her hand, she held a recruitment flier of her own, giving her strength when a part of her wanted to fall apart. The parchment rattled in her grip, and she forced herself to take a deep breath to steady her nerves.

She caught sight of Mrs. Keats outside the inn near the back, washing sheets in a large outdoor wash bin. The methodic scrub, dunk, and scrub some more helped ease some of her nerves.

As she approached, she stuffed the parchment into her pocket and returned the woman's smile.

"Well, if it isn't Mirabelle herself. I never thought I'd see you loitering around the inn again." The woman winked, causing a wicked blush to flare in her cheeks. "To what do I owe the pleasure of your visit?"

Without asking permission, Mirabelle snatched one of the dirtied sheets and dunked it into the water, falling into her own repetitive movements as she scrubbed the white material with lye soap.

"I wanted to speak with you, actually." She felt Mrs. Keats' stare but focused on the work instead. "I—"

"Look who it is!" Jeremy shouted across the yard from where he exited the inn with more sheets in his hands, followed by Gilberd close at his heels. "And not a moment too soon."

Jeremy pushed Gilberd in their direction with a shove to the shoulder. Mirabelle's breath caught. Gilberd had shaved.

Heat spiked in her blood as her gaze roamed over his face, but mostly over the strong jaw leading to a muscled, attractive neck, which had been hidden beneath facial hair for weeks. *And that scar.*

She slowly reached for a cloth napkin from the pile in the basket and fanned her flaming face while holding his grinning gaze. Gilberd Keats wasn't just big and rugged and corded with thick muscles. He was handsome. Moreso with a clean-shaven face. The scar on his jaw accentuated the attention his presence demanded. Large. Rough. Capable. And far too handsome for his own good.

An ache settled in her heart. Because she had to make a sacrifice she didn't want to make. But if she didn't sacrifice, then he would. And she would never forgive herself for it.

"Hmm." Gilberd dropped a pile of linens beside the wash tub while folding his arms, his eyes shining with an inevitable jest. "I seem to remember a beautiful lady promising to run in my direction should I shave." He made a show of glancing around. "As it is, there are no ladies running in my direction at all."

"Oh, Gil." Mrs. Keats laughed, reaching up to pat his cheek. It looked soft, and she wanted to touch it herself. "Such a teasing flirt. Go make yourself useful, will you? I need more firewood stacked in the kitchen."

"Fine." He sighed dramatically. "But to think I spent all that time shaving this morning, and no one appreciates it."

He moved to pass her, but she grabbed onto his hand and pulled him down to her level. Not caring who witnessed it, she kissed him on his soft cheek, just over his scar, and whispered in his ear. "I appreciate it."

Hope flickered in his eyes, followed by something else she couldn't quite read. Although he said nothing about the exchange, she noticed his gaze continuously darting toward her while he fulfilled his mother's request for transporting firewood from the shed to the kitchen.

Gilberd disappeared inside for a few moments. Mirabelle took that allotted time to speak, her words escaping in a rush.

"Mrs. Keats—"

"Please call me Beatrice." The woman's smile hadn't faded since Mirabelle had kissed her son.

She stood to drape a sheet over the clothesline, attempting to collect her thoughts. Finally, she tried again, "Beatrice, my father is growing more ill. I need medicine to take away some of his pains."

"I have some right inside—"

"You misheard me," she interrupted, staring purposefully into her eyes right as Gilberd passed them again. "I need some strong medicine. I've heard there is a very good apothecary in Edilann."

Slowly, the woman's eyes widened as she finally caught onto her meaning. All too quickly, she schooled her expression, her gaze darting toward her son. "I'm not in possession of the right herbs. Usually, I send Gilberd on those trips." She motioned for him to join them. "Gil, I need you to journey to Edilann to visit an apothecary for me. It's for Mr. Waters, you see. So, you will need to make haste."

Gilberd raised an eyebrow. "Now? That will be at least a week's roundtrip." He glanced at Mirabelle. "What about the apothecary here?"

"They don't have exactly what I need."

He scratched his head and then ran a hand over his mouth. "What about the ranch?" he asked, turning his attention to her. "I don't want you to handle it on your own."

"I will be fine." She touched his arm reassuringly. "You already took care of the hard parts. I'll survive without you." When he still didn't look convinced, she gently squeezed his forearm. "Really."

His defiance faltered. "Are you sure?"

"Yes."

After studying her for several long moments, he finally nodded. "I will get ready for the journey then. I'll leave first thing in the morning."

He turned and strode back toward the inn, and the moment he disappeared, Mirabelle closed her eyes and sighed, willing her emotions to steady within her. The feat proved difficult. Once in Edilann, she knew he wouldn't be able to resist the pull of tryouts. When he left Millbrook, she knew she might not see him for many more weeks to come. Possibly even months.

"You are so good to him." Beatrice squeezed her hand and spoke quietly as if not wanting to be overheard, even though Gilberd was inside. "He will thank you for this."

"I can see how much he wants this." Her gaze traveled to the empty doorway. "I couldn't live with myself if I made him throw that away for me. But do you think getting him there is enough?"

The woman's brows furrowed with worry. "It needs to be enough because it's all we can do. He will have to do the rest."

Gilberd appeared around the corner carrying a knapsack in his arms, and he cast her a coy look despite his mother standing by her side. The moment he ventured back into the kitchen, she spoke again.

"It's not much for the herbs," she whispered as she handed several coins to Beatrice. "But it's all I have."

Beatrice shook her head and handed them back, saying in an equal whisper, "*Family* never pays." Her meaning came across loud and clear. Mirabelle would be a part of this family. Not now, but eventually. In her heart, she knew it to be true.

Tears threatened to fall, and she turned more fully away from the window where Gilberd was visible to hide them from him. "How can I miss him so much already?" She sniffed quietly and surreptitiously dabbed at the corners of her eyes with her sleeve.

"Because love has enough power to wound even the strongest of souls." The woman squeezed her hand but then raised her voice as Gilberd passed by once again. "Don't forget your sword, dear. I don't want you to be defenseless against bandits."

"I wouldn't dream of leaving without it. I'm not sure how useful I'd be but the least I can do is try." He stopped and pointed at her. "I'll come by later to cover the hay outside. Just in case it rains."

Her chin wobbled. She didn't want to say goodbye to him yet. "And the ladder. You promised to get it down for me from the hayloft."

Gilberd snorted and shook his head. "Your father is great, honestly. But that is a poor place to store a spare ladder."

When he disappeared again, Mirabelle took a steadying breath. How had she survived weeks without him? She'd come to rely on him far too much within the last few days. But she was strong and resilient, fully capable of running the ranch on her own for a short while.

Unease rippled through her when she spotted a familiar figure standing across the street, flask in hand, as he stared unabashedly at her with possessiveness in his eyes. Barnaby took a swig from the flask and leaned back against a fence post.

She quickly ducked her head to hide herself in the mountains of laundry, but she knew he'd seen her.

A tremor started from her toes and traveled its way up her spine and into her fingers. If Gilberd left Millbrook, would Barnaby start harassing her again?

But when she glanced up, he was gone.

Uttering a hasty farewell to Beatrice, Mirabelle's feet found their way to the road, and she quickened her step when she reached the road sign where the path forked left. Despite glancing over her shoulder several times, she found no sign of Barnaby in pursuit. And when she reached her property, she breathed easier within the safety of home.

Still, she counted down the minutes until Gilberd should arrive, if only to feel his safe, comforting presence by her side.

A heaviness weighed on Gilberd's mind, his thoughts distracted as he focused on his trip to Edilann tomorrow. Journeying to the big city wasn't unusual, as there were supplies his parents often needed or shipments to be picked up. Of course, he didn't want to leave Mirabelle for a single day, and leaving her for at least a week pained him.

Yes, all of that distracted him as he secured the covering around the large stack of hay. But what distracted him most was the thought of running into men dressed in armor and weapons, standing before the king as they pledged their allegiance to his army. He didn't want to watch it. He didn't want to be anywhere near the city right now.

But he also wanted it almost more than anything.

"Argh!" he groaned, kicking a bale of hay at the bottom of the stack.

For a moment, he entertained the thought of becoming a soldier, making his own wage as he cared for Mirabelle, their children, and even her parents in Edilann. Everything he'd ever wanted lay within reach for once in his life, but it wasn't the right time.

He wasn't sure it would ever be.

"If you are done fighting with the bales," Mirabelle said, startling him out of his thoughts, "I could use some help with the ladder."

She held a lantern in her hand, a warm, orange glow casting shadows across her lovely features. He could easily imagine himself looking into her eyes at the end of each day and bidding her a goodnight before she blew out the candle and they fell asleep in each other's arms.

But…

One week.

She said she'd wait for him. And although he wasn't going to Edilann to join the army but to buy medicine, he still feared she might change her mind after so long of his absence.

An irrational fear of losing her spun his mind until he felt uncomfortably dizzy. But it was only a week, maybe less if he hurried. There was no need for this level of intense fear to churn within him.

To try to hide it, he offered a smile and followed her into the barn. A nicker greeted them when they entered, bringing his attention to the horse and milking cow inside their stables on one side of the barn. On the other side lay stacks of hay and equipment for taking care of the ranch and the animals. A loft rested in front of them, dividing a fourth of the barn in half.

In an agile movement, he used a nail jutting out from the wall as a foothold as he reached up and grabbed the edge of the loft. With his other hand, he latched onto the ladder and pulled it out of its resting place and leaned it against the wall.

Without preamble, Mirabelle began to climb, and he couldn't help but admire her figure with a goofy grin on his face. At least until she glanced over her shoulder and raised an eyebrow at him.

"I was going to show you a magnificent view," she teased, "but it seems you already found one."

He burst into laughter and shook his head, following her up the ladder until they reached the loft. A layer of dust caked the surface of several crates and the wooden floorboards. He covered his nose with his elbow to keep from sneezing when the stale air tickled his nostrils.

Mirabelle opened the window shutters, sat backward on the ledge, and his heart gave a start when she climbed out and disappeared from sight.

"Mira!" he gasped as he rushed after her, but a wave of relief washed over him when he found a sturdy, safe-enough ladder attached to the side of the barn. He followed her up this ladder as well until they crested over the edge and settled down beside each other on stiff shingles.

"You know how I feel about roofs," he said in a stern tone, an uneasiness crawling over him as he surveyed the distance from the roof to the ground. It was an even greater height than the house.

"Uh huh." She turned her head to rest on her shoulder and cast him a flirtatious grin. "That they're a good place for stolen kisses."

Oh, he wanted to kiss her until they were both dizzy. Though, the roof wasn't the best place for a spinning head. "Just promise me you won't get on the roof while I'm gone. I don't want to worry about you falling."

The mention of him leaving seemed to deflate her mood, and she hugged her arms around her knees, her chin resting on top.

He wrapped an arm around her shoulders and pulled her into his side, and wordlessly, they stared out over the horizon. His breath caught at the numerous stars shining over their heads. At the faint silhouette of the mountains in the distance framed by a golden-orange glow. At the breathtaking scenery he'd seen all his life but never truly stopped to appreciate.

Unable to stay quiet for long, he said, "I must hand it to you. This is the second-best view I've seen in the past ten minutes."

She elbowed him in the ribs but smiled anyway and snuggled closer to him. He loved the way she fit beneath his arm, against his side, her head resting perfectly against his chest. Ten years ago, he'd never been able to imagine himself in this position. Rather than teasing her, he was loving her.

Love.

He hid his smile in her hair as the warm emotion burned bright in his soul. If his mother hadn't tried to make a match of them, would they have done the deed themselves? Or would they have passed each other by, never to cross paths even in the small town?

Although he wanted to shout his love for her from the rooftops, he was no fool. Their relationship was fragile, easily breakable. Untested. Untried. He didn't want to bend it too far lest it shatter.

"I should go home," he said against her soft hair. "I just don't want to say goodbye to you yet."

She lifted her head until they gazed into each other's eyes, and his heart melted a bit more beneath her heated stare. "We don't need to say goodbye with words."

A flutter raced through his chest at the insinuation, and like he thought before, he was no fool. He would take what she would give.

"Just one kiss."

One kiss turned into two, which turned into three. And soon enough, he lost count and instead fell headfirst into the sweetness of her lips and the romantic atmosphere surrounding them. He loved this woman. And he would do everything he could to prove it to her each day.

"*D* *on't open it until you're halfway to Edilann,*" Mirabelle had warned as she'd handed him a sealed envelope.

"And I mean it. Believe me, I'll be able to feel you opening it if you do it too early."

Gilberd smiled wistfully as the wagon jostled him back and forth with every dip in the road. He turned the small envelope in his hands, running his finger from corner to corner as he itched to tear it open. Only a few more minutes until he reached the midpoint.

At last, when a large pond passed by on the right side of the road, he slid his finger beneath the seal and opened the envelope. A piece of parchment lay inside. His eagerness proved far stronger than his embarrassment as he unfolded it and stared back at a paragraph filled with words. He peered at the letter for far too long as he sounded out each word in his head until it finally made sense.

Dearest Gilberd,

Just like how you pushed me into a closet because you were afraid to kiss me, I'm sending you with a letter because I am afraid to say these things in person.

Laughter escaped his mouth, gathering the attention of the five other passengers on the wagon with him. Two squares lay at the bottom of the page, one with the word "no" over it and the other "yes."

It read: *Will you court me? Check yes or no.*

Another chuckle escaped him, and he didn't hesitate to check yes using a piece of charcoal hidden inside the envelope. It was so juvenile. As if they were children again. But he loved it. He loved her. He wanted to spend the rest of his life with her.

He rubbed his thumb along the bottom of the page where she ended with *Forever, Mirabelle.* He was such a lucky, lucky man.

After placing the letter back into his knapsack for safe keeping, he surveyed his surroundings as they passed. Thick green trees. Flickers of sunlight across a large pond. Travelers passing to the side of them, some on horses and others on foot.

"Do you think we'll get to see Prince Sterling?" one of the little girls giggled across from him, perhaps age eight or nine. "I barely caught a glimpse of him last time. There were so many guards."

The girl's mother patted her head. "The king is supposed to make an appearance at tryouts. I don't think the prince will be there."

"Why not?" The innocence in the girl's large eyes nearly made him chuckle, but he didn't want them to think he was eavesdropping. Not that he had a choice when they sat directly across from him.

"Because he's sickly," the older brother said, around age fifteen, and Gilberd couldn't help but notice the sword resting in his lap as if he were trying out for the army himself. "That's why he never goes out."

"That's not true," the older sister argued, probably a couple of years older than the boy. "He's the heir and only child. That's why they don't let him out of the castle. He could die. And then what?"

The siblings continued to squabble over the state of the young prince. Gilberd had never seen Prince Sterling himself, but he was bound to be around ten years old.

He sighed and pulled his attention away and toward the long stretch of road ahead of them. The army and the royal family were none of his business. Not anymore. Maybe someday, though unlikely, he'd find himself wielding a sword and fighting in the name of good and justice. Fighting for his kingdom. For his family. For his freedom and others' safety.

He fingered the pommel of his sword tied to his belt, running his palm down the sheath with a longing for adventure away from the small town of Millbrook burning in his soul.

I can be something more. Something greater.

But another part of him whispered, *You already are great. You don't need anything more.*

Because with Mirabelle at his side, he wasn't left wanting.

"Are you going to the recruitment?" the young man asked suddenly, and it took a few moments to realize he spoke to him.

Gilberd shook his head. "No. I have an errand to run in the city."

"Well, why not? You look the part."

He chuckled. Yes, sometimes he felt silly waiting tables and changing bed sheets as big as he was. But... "Just an errand," he repeated, and the young man turned his attention back to his sisters.

Along the journey, they'd picked up several more passengers and stopped for one more night on the side of the road to sleep rather than in a rickety wagon. The next day as they resumed their journey, an abundance of armored men on horseback made an appearance the closer they came to the city. Some were even younger than the boy riding in the wagon with him while others were old enough to be his grandfather.

The rich scent of tanned hides and metallic armor greeted him like a punch of nostalgia, if only in his mind. The clamor of swords reached his ears when they entered the city at last, even louder than shopkeepers haggling their wares in the crowded marketplace.

A plethora of people slowed the wagon's progress until it halted altogether within the sea of color and excitement.

Having paid for the ride in advance, Gilberd hopped out of the stationary wagon and joined the throng of people while keeping his belongings close to his person. The big city might be crawling with guards and soldiers, but thieves still ran about beneath his nose.

Straight to the apothecary, he chanted in his mind, keeping his focus forward rather than letting it wander. *Buy the herbs. Board the wagon. Return home.*

But his gaze *did* wander when he spotted an acrobat twirling fire on a baton. The flaming baton moved so quickly that it looked like a circle rather than a stick. The audience "oohed" and "ahhed" when he threw the spinning baton in the air and clapped when he caught it without burning himself.

I wouldn't mind living here, his mind whispered before he managed to halt the thought in its tracks.

He forced himself to pull away from the gathered crowd and continued on his way toward the apothecary booth in a market crowded enough to make moving difficult. Some people took in his size and moved immediately. Others stared at him curiously as he passed, likely wondering if he was joining the army.

His feet scuffled along the cobblestone path until he managed to reach the wooden booth filled with hanging dried herbs and other items laid out on the rectangular table. He waited in line until his feet protested over standing for so long.

Finally, he reached the front of the line, completed his purchase, and safely tucked the herbs away.

Away from the apothecary, he chanted again. *Board the wagon. Return home.*

But then he saw it.

The training grounds were filled with people from soldiers to aspiring guardsmen to wide-eyed boys. Spectators gathered around a wooden fence to watch soldiers train and fight and prove themselves on a field that stretched almost as far as the eye could see. And like a gnat unable to resist the pull of the flame, he joined the crowd.

Soldiers fought weapon against weapon while a commandeering man walked slowly around the field, likely the captain of the guard judging by the blue cloak pinned to his breast by the royal emblem—crossed halberds surrounded by a laurel wreath.

The captain corrected postures, fixed fighting techniques, and dismissed lacking recruits while accepting others.

He tightened his grip on the pommel of his sword as he wondered how he might fare on the training grounds. All he needed to do was talk to the recruitment officer in front of the field and prove himself. He didn't need to accept a soldier position if offered. It was more than likely he'd be dismissed because of his lack of formal training.

Seemingly without his consent, his feet began moving in the direction of the recruitment officer. But then he stopped and squeezed his eyes shut as he remembered Mirabelle, her extensive ranch, and her ailing father.

He couldn't afford to waste time dallying on the field playing soldier for a day.

The disappointment burned him from the inside out as if he'd swallowed the acrobat's entire flaming baton. But this was for the best. Truly, it was.

Gilberd frowned when he spotted three men with stiff postures, huddled far too closely together as they stood off to the side of the crowd of spectators. They threw off their Edilann-blue cloaks, and one of the men pulled an Armandy-red cloak out of a bag—

"Sterling? Sterling! Where are you?"

His attention snapped toward the sound of the woman's voice, only for his heart to jolt in surprise. Both the king and queen had made an appearance at the training grounds today. Guards flocked them as they walked about the square wearing fine clothes and silver crowns atop their heads.

However, worry pinched the king's mouth and the queen's expression was frantic.

They were searching for the prince.

When Gilberd was ten years old, he would have been standing at the front of the wooden fence watching the soldiers fight with awe-filled wonder in his eyes. So, he scanned the fence post closely and spotted a smaller figure with a blue cloak shrouding his face and body as if trying not to stand out in the crowd. But the fine shoes peeking out from beneath the cloak gave him away.

"He's over here!" Gilberd shouted and pointed toward the prince, but the din of the crowd swallowed his voice. He waved his hands to try to get their attention but neither the king or queen nor their guards glanced his way. The thought of approaching them or even the prince caused a pit of discomfort to grow in his belly. One didn't speak to royalty without permission, right?

Deciding to approach the boy, he turned but his heart leaped into his throat when the three figures now wearing red rushed toward the prince with swords drawn, the weapons hidden beneath the cloaks. The intent in their eyes was unmistakable.

They were here to assassinate the prince.

Gilberd reacted quickly, hardly thinking as he drew his sword, pushing people out of his way as he raced toward Sterling, who continued to stare out into the training field. The first assassin swung his weapon, aiming at the boy's neck. Someone screamed. Gilberd lunged forward. The tip of his sword grazed the other weapon just enough to thwart its path. The blade missed its target and instead embedded itself into the wooden fence.

His body moved faster than his mind as he twisted to the side and thrust his weapon into the assassin's chest, coming back bloody.

And then the screams began in earnest.

The second assassin attempted the next move, aiming for Sterling's chest right as he spun around with wide blue eyes. Gilberd grabbed the hood of the boy's cloak and yanked hard enough for the blade to miss by a hair's breadth. Sterling crashed to the ground and curled into a fetal position, hands protecting his head.

Gilberd stepped over him, using himself as his shield as he parried attacks coming from two different sides, all while spectators screamed and darted away from the danger. He barely managed to block an overhand blow before spinning to knock the other man's sword to the side as he attempted to jab at Sterling.

His blood rushed to his ears, every inch of his body on high alert as he swung, parried, blocked, and swung again. Screeching metal and clanging weapons seemed to fill every inch of his head. If he didn't end this quickly, he, Sterling, or both of them would die.

One of the assassins brought his sword down over his head, and being taller, Gilberd blocked it and kicked the man in the knee to knock him off balance. Bones cracked. The man howled. And with the small opening, Gilberd swung his weapon fast and struck him across the torso.

The man slumped onto the ground unmoving.

He ducked as he heard the last blade whip toward him, but not fast enough. The tip of the weapon skimmed the surface of his hairline beside his temple. Blood rushed down the side of his face and dripped off his chin, but he never once let his gaze stray from the enemy assassin.

With only one opponent left, each of Gilberd's swings were fast and hard to force the other man backward. Though, he didn't dare step away from the prince in case one of the other two felled assassins managed another attack after their grave injuries.

His sword sliced his opponent's thigh, bringing him down to one knee. In a few maneuvers, he disarmed the assassin. The blade flew through the air and clattered across dirt and loose rocks.

And then the blood stopped rushing through his ears long enough for him to make sense of a hundred movements at once. The screams entered his ears in earnest. Edilann guards rushed forward to help Sterling to his feet while several others apprehended the third living assassin. The king and queen stared at him with shock in their eyes before the queen burst into tears and pulled Sterling into her embrace, kissing every inch of his face.

Gilberd's attention slipped toward his bloodied sword, and shock coursed through his body like the frigid water of a mountain stream.

He dropped his weapon to show he meant no harm, and only then did King Royce approach with several guards flanking him.

"Who are you?" the man gasped, his gaze shooting from his shoes to his bloodied shirt to the blood running from his hairline. He produced a handkerchief from his pocket, and Gilberd gratefully accepted, wincing as he pressed it against his wound.

"Just an innkeeper's son." He barely managed to remember to bow before his king. "Your Highness."

"Surely not with how you handle a blade." But then fury flashed across his expression as his gaze shot up, and everyone within the vicinity fell into a hush. "There are two thousand soldiers here!" the king thundered. "And no one thought to protect my son? Your next king?"

Murmurs of apologies surrounded them, followed by shameful hanging of heads.

To be fair, it was more than likely no one had noticed Sterling. Otherwise, this scenario may have played out differently. But he didn't dare interrupt his king to state as much.

King Royce gripped his shoulder, thoroughly shocking him with the touch. "You saved my son's life. He is my only child. My heir." The man swallowed before releasing him. "Come with me to the palace. I would like a private word with you."

The order showered him in dread as he cleaned the blood from his sword on a patch of grass and placed the weapon inside his scabbard. An entourage of guards surrounded them on all sides, but what surprised him most was that none of the guards positioned themselves between him and the royal family.

Young Sterling continuously glanced his way, the intensity of his blue eyes filled with both horror and curiosity. The boy remained quiet, not uttering a single word as they made their way back toward the castle on foot.

The journey didn't last long, and soon he found himself staring up at towering blocks of stone with spires housing the blue and gold Edilann flags at the top. They flapped in a gentle breeze, a reminder of whose palace he was about to enter.

Trying to disguise a shuddering breath as a cough, he followed the entourage up several stone steps leading to the double-doored entrance guarded by men holding spears. Queen Claudia led Prince Sterling down a small corridor but not before the boy cast one last glance in his direction.

Several guards escorted the king to what appeared to be a dining room with a long table set with glasses, plates, and silverware. Blue and gold banners hung from the ceiling and nearly brushed the floor, woven with Edilann's royal crest on each tapestry. A half-dozen windows lined one wall while decorative weapons lined another.

But then he jumped when the doors shut with a resounding *bang*, leaving the king and himself by their lonesome.

Gilberd dropped the handkerchief from his head to fiddle with his sleeve as he stared back at the powerful man in front of him. Wavy brown hair adorned with a silver crown. Eyes as blue as Sterling's. Fine clothing and an even finer weapon at his side.

"I mean no disrespect…but should there not be a guard with you in here?"

The king gave him a pointed look. "If you cannot be alone with *me*, how can I allow you to be alone with my son?"

"I don't…understand."

He scratched his head but winced when his fingers brushed against his wound. It no longer bled, which meant the injury wasn't as terrible as it seemed.

King Royce approached until only the corner of the dining table lay between them. "You single-handedly saved my son from three assassins. No one else bothered to jump in to help when they very well could have."

"I spotted Prince Sterling moments before the attack. Anyone else in my position would have done something."

"*No one* did anything. Except you. In the same position, I don't believe anyone would have reacted as quickly as you did. Sterling isn't even your charge, and you put your life on the line for him."

Gilberd lowered his gaze, not knowing what to say. His body had reacted to the danger, the first time he'd ever been put in such a situation as to need to protect someone's life. How could he take credit for instinct?

The king continued, "I would like to offer you a guardsman position. Prince Sterling as your charge."

He blinked several times, his mouth slowly falling open as he tried to discern if he'd heard the king correctly. "What? Are you… Why would…" He shook his head in disbelief at the man's expectant stare. "I don't have any extensive education. Besides, I have a life. A family."

But like a man used to getting his way, the king continued to persuade, "Travel with us to Oxenberg. We leave tomorrow for the wedding. It will only be for a couple of days. If you decide this isn't the right job for you, you can return home. But if you decide the fit is right, the position is yours."

The mix of shock and disbelief spun his surroundings until his legs could no longer bear his weight. He sank into a chair and held a hand to his aching head as he thought about Mirabelle and how this might affect her. How it might affect *them*. This was the best offer he could ever take, far better than the position of a soldier. But guarding the *prince*? How could he accept such a hefty responsibility?

Finally, he lifted his gaze to find the king watching him closely, the expectant stare still lingering in his eyes. "Why me? You overestimate my station if you think this is something I am qualified for."

A sigh escaped the king's lips, and he lowered himself into a chair adjacent to him and poured himself a drink from the pitcher on the table. After the assassination attempt earlier, Gilberd silently cautioned against drinking anything that had been unattended for any length of time. But the man didn't keel over from poison.

"Sterling has been going through a rebellious phase," King Royce said quietly as he sipped at his drink. "He has been sneaking out with no caution for his own life or his title. He doesn't care for the throne, and I fear he might try to run away altogether."

A pause followed his words, but nothing more of an explanation escaped the king's mouth. "And what can I do about it?" Gilberd finally asked, tiptoeing the line between respectful subject and wary confidante.

"If he's determined to sneak out, then he will no matter what I say. If I keep him locked inside, he'll only grow to resent me and the crown." The king traced his eyebrow with a weary sigh. "Your job will be to accompany him wherever he goes, whether he knows it or not. You will be the shadow he becomes familiar with as he grows up. Someone he can trust. Someone who is capable of protecting him even with his own life." And then his eyes bore into his. Begging. Pleading. "I will pay you *handsomely* to accept this position. I will provide housing, weapons, a wage."

"I don't have any weapons training."

"Hah," the king scoffed. "Says the man who took down three assassins by himself while protecting his charge." He took another long sip of his drink, and Gilberd highly suspected it wasn't water. "But if you believe you need more training, I will provide it."

Gilberd pinched the bridge of his nose, knowing he would never get another opportunity like this again. This was more than he could have ever hoped for. Not just a soldier, but a personal guard. The weight of the king's trust burned in his soul, and he wanted to prove himself worthy of it.

But what about Mirabelle?

He opened his eyes to find the king watching him again as if ready to try another persuasion tactic should he try to refuse. But he wouldn't. Because he was no fool. Surely, everything would work out. Mirabelle would support him in his decision, wouldn't she?

Finally, he nodded. "I accept the position. Though, I have a woman waiting at home. I'll have to return for her."

"Of course." King Royce's eyes gleamed with triumph. "After the journey to Oxenberg, I will give you two weeks to tie up all your loose ends. It's only fair."

They shook hands as Gilberd said, "You are very generous, Sire."

"You saved my son's life. There is not enough *generosity* in the world to repay you for what you have done today." He gestured toward the door. "I will have a room made up for you and send someone to debrief you, so you are fully aware of what is expected of your position."

Gilberd nodded gratefully. "I appreciate your trust, Your Highness. I swear I won't let you or Prince Sterling down."

The king returned his nod and stood, though Gilberd didn't miss the slight tremor in the man's hands as if recovering from the shock of almost losing his only child. "Supper is a few hours away. I expect your presence as a guard."

His gaze turned toward the window, and though he would never be able to spot the silhouette of Millbrook from here, his heart lay with the woman who resided there. "I need to send a letter first."

Never in his life had Gilberd felt so out of place.

Clomping horse hooves filled his ears as the king's entourage traveled down a wide path with shady green trees on either side of them. A dozen soldiers accompanied the royal family where they rode on their mounts between the protection of their guards. The king and queen rode side by side on the path large enough to comfortably accommodate two horses.

And Sterling…

He rode by himself, his expression blank and withdrawn. He seemed…unhappy. Perhaps even lonely. It was any wonder the child kept acting insubordinate and had run away from home on multiple occasions.

Not once had Gilberd heard the boy speak since his arrival. Sterling was forbidden from stepping outside after the assassination attempt, even with guards at his side. They'd sequestered him in his room with piles of books and a stuffy old tutor who couldn't see how many fingers he was holding up unless he put his hand directly in front of the man's face.

Something had to change. If King Royce truly wanted Sterling to step up and embrace his responsibilities as the heir to the throne, then he needed to allow the boy some freedom.

The guard beside him continued his lessons in quiet tones, pulling Gilberd's attention away from Sterling.

"You must always follow him at a distance," the man instructed. "But remain close enough to aid him if necessary."

"Always?" How lonely.

He studied Sterling again and noticed the hunch in his shoulders. His expression remained blank, but the faintest downward curve of his mouth gave the young prince away. This was not a happy child. He had no friends and little freedom.

Gilberd wanted to be more than a shadow. He wanted to be as close to a friend as he was able to despite their fifteen-year age difference and the vast valley of rank between them.

Ignoring the guard's words, he spurred his horse forward until he rode beside Sterling rather than behind. The boy glanced at him from the corner of his eye, but otherwise did nothing more. The same spark of curiosity entered his expression like from the day before.

Several minutes of silence passed aside from snorting horses, clomping hooves, and whispered conversations between the king and queen. But they didn't object to him riding near Sterling like this, so he dared to speak.

He patted his horse's neck. "Have you ever played 'Spy the Color?'"

The prince didn't reply, but his cautious curiosity transitioned into wariness. He doubted the servants and guards at the castle spoke to him.

Not one to give up easily, Gilberd delved headfirst into the game. "I am looking for something the color blue."

Although Sterling said nothing, his gaze flickered to the sky.

"All right, so that one was easy. Let's give you more of a challenge." He chuckled, delighted when he'd captured the prince's attention easier than expected. "I'm looking for something the color orange."

Still no words from the prince, but his gaze jumped about until it landed on two orange and green birds flitting over a nest in the treetops. A smile slowly spread across the boy's lips, and the tension in his shoulders relaxed considerably.

"Now, I'm looking for the color red."

Sterling spent several minutes on this next challenge, his eyebrows drawn, and his lips puckered in concentration. Finally, his eyes lit up when his mother lifted a hand to tuck a strand of hair behind her ear, revealing the ruby ring on her finger.

"That one was hard!" Sterling laughed, surprising him with the joy in his voice from such a simple interaction. The sound of his voice even seemed to startle the king and queen, as they turned in their saddles to stare incredulously at their son. "I'm looking for something green. But it's not a plant or a tree."

"The grass?"

The prince shook his head. "Not the grass either."

"My doublet."

"No. It's too easy."

Gilberd ran a hand over the bristles on his chin as he searched the vicinity for something green. Two more green and orange birds flitted past, but he crossed them off his mental list, thinking Sterling wouldn't pick an object they'd already used.

He guessed moss, vines, and buttons, but each were wrong. But then he spotted the green face of one of the guards ahead of them. His mouth twitched in amusement as he nodded his head toward the poor chap.

"Is motion sickness on your list?"

Sterling burst into laughter, but when his parents' mouths practically dropped to the ground as they spun around again in shock, the boy quickly sobered as he shut his mouth and stared at his saddle.

So *this* had been what the king had been referring to. Not just defiance against his position as heir to the kingdom, but the desire to close off entirely when around others. He supposed being unhappy in life would likely spur the prince into wanting to run away from home.

A thick wall surrounded Sterling's ten-year-old heart, and Gilberd was determined to break through it.

As if realizing what their sudden attention had done to their son, the king and queen turned back around to stare ahead, but not before sharing a concerned look with one another.

Several more minutes of silence passed, and Gilberd suddenly realized how difficult his position would be. He was not a quiet man by any means. Keeping his mouth shut would prove to be a challenge for him. However, he was determined to make this work, especially because he was beginning to care about his new charge. He wanted Sterling to be happy and comfortable.

The guard ahead of them turned sharply in his saddle, startling his horse into jerking to the side as he vomited onto the ground. Gilberd and Sterling shared an amused look, and the boy clamped a hand over his mouth as if to try to keep himself from laughing again.

Prince Sterling didn't speak again for the rest of the journey to Oxenberg, but his expression was lighter, and his mouth turned upward in a near-smile. It was a start, and Gilberd fully planned to continue his efforts throughout their acquaintance.

Mirabelle wrung her hands as she watched the road from where she stood in the market square. Soldiers on horseback passed. Two wagons creaked by, though none of them carried Gilberd. And plenty of people filled the market, haggling and purchasing food and supplies.

Gilberd was supposed to be coming home today. She desperately hoped he would. She also desperately hoped he wouldn't.

"The stress is eating you, too?" Beatrice Keats asked as she approached and stood beside her as they both watched the road. Any minute now. Surely.

But when what she suspected might have been Gilberd's wagon passed and several passengers stepped down, her heart deflated when he wasn't on board.

A breath shuddered from her lungs at what his absence meant. He wasn't coming home. And she hated not knowing how long he might be gone. But she had sent him there, fully expecting him to find himself and live his dreams. Now she needed to accept the reality that everything might change for them for the worse.

As if sensing her downtrodden spirit, Beatrice squeezed her hand, offering no words but only her presence as comfort.

Her heart picked up again with hope when the Millbrook's postman sifted through several envelopes as he approached. He handed an envelope to Beatrice, and her heart soared when she noticed the return address from Gilberd.

And then her heart stuttered entirely when he handed another letter to her before departing. Her hands shook, afraid to find out what lay within but eager all the same. She watched Beatrice open her envelope first. It contained a short letter.

And the requested herbs.

He wasn't returning.

Mirabelle placed a hand against her dizzy head and reached out to the nearby empty stall to steady herself. How had she so thoroughly become smitten with the man? She could no longer imagine a life without him, and suddenly realizing she might lose him entirely struck fear in her heart.

Her fingers shook as she opened her letter, dreading what she might find within its contents. Two separate papers slid out—the letter she wrote him and another he wrote himself. On her letter, the "yes" box was checked, and she sighed with relief before she managed a laugh.

Placing her heart on the line, no matter how juvenile, terrified her. But she was entirely relieved he wanted the same things as her.

She carefully unfolded the second letter and first noticed the messy handwriting, silently wondering how long it took Gilberd to write it. From what she'd gathered over the weeks, she knew he struggled with reading and even more with writing. But he'd made an effort for her, and she appreciated it more than he could possibly know.

My Lovely Mirabelle,

I miss you with every fiber of my heart. I wish I could come back home to see you. But… Something has happened. I cannot say yet what it is, but I promise it's a good thing. I hope. I'm nervous about what you might think and how we can make this work.

I will be returning home in a week. Though, it will likely be only a few days after you receive my letter.
With love,
Gil

"He did it," she breathed, closing her eyes and holding the letter to her heart when she wasn't sure if she would shout for joy or weep with heartache. "He joined the army."

She handed the letter to Beatrice, whose smile wavered with emotion as she read the words. "As a mother, I'm terrified. But I'm also proud. All I want is for him to be happy and safe."

Mirabelle nodded in agreement as she accepted the letter back, though discomfort churned in her belly as she thought of what it meant to possibly be the wife of a soldier one day. She'd always worry about whether he would return home. She would also worry if their children would find themselves fatherless. She hated the feeling of the unknown. But she loved Gilberd. Facing the terrifying unknown with him was worth it just to have him in her life.

"My mother needs me back at the ranch," she said as she tucked the letter safely away into her pocket. "Hopefully, we will see each other again in a few days."

Beatrice gave her a warm smile and a motherly hug before Mirabelle sauntered back toward the ranch, her heart lighter than only minutes prior. All week, she had agonized over what her future might bring. But now she knew.

And she would make it work.

With feet floating on air, she almost didn't notice the black horse saddled and secured to a wooden fence post around the bend to her house. She stopped in her tracks, her heart pounding, before she spun around and darted in the opposite direction.

But then someone grabbed her around the waist and clamped a hand over her mouth as she released a scream. His glove muffled the sound.

She kicked and screamed and struggled but it was as if she were a sack of bucking flour with the way her efforts landed her nowhere.

Her captor dragged her through tall, thick grass and through a thicket of dense trees until they reached the river, where her screams were garbled up and swallowed by the raucous water.

The man spun her around and pinned her against the tree, and a plume of alcoholic breath wafted in her face, a pair of light blue eyes staring menacingly down at her. She tried to fight back against Barnaby's grip, but the more she struggled, the tighter he held her.

The foul stench of his breath made her gag, and she managed to turn her head away from him but nothing more.

"I. *Own*. You." Barnaby punctuated each word, repeating what he'd said weeks earlier before she'd fallen into the river.

"You don't own me, you dirty pig!"

She stomped on his foot. But the attack only angered him, and he tightened his grip on her until tears of pain smarted in her eyes and an involuntary whimper escaped her mouth.

"I don't want to hurt you," he said in a threatening tone. "But I am getting tired of this. You will marry me. You don't have a choice."

"Get your filthy hands off me!"

"Your father sold you to me to pay off his debt!"

Mirabelle stopped struggling, her eyes slowly widening as she turned to stare at the awful man before her. She blinked several times, recalling the strange conversations she'd had with her father within the past month. He'd admitted to being in a lot of debt, but she'd assumed it was all in his head.

"Pardon?" she gasped.

Finally, Barnaby released her, and as if satisfied she wouldn't try to run again, he reached into his pocket and pulled out a stack of folded documents, handing them to her.

Dread dribbled from her chest and dropped to her toes as she read through the documents. When Edilann's economy had crashed, her father had taken out a loan from Barnaby's father to keep the ranch going, clearly with the expectation of paying off his debts quickly. But when he hadn't, he'd taken out a second loan but only with the promise that if he didn't pay back the money, Mirabelle, her mother, and the entire ranch would belong to Barnaby and his father.

Her hand fluttered over her mouth as the horror of what her father had done stared back at her, along with his barely legible signature beneath each official document.

"But he's on his deathbed!" she cried, glancing up to find smug satisfaction in Barnaby's eyes. "He cannot pay off these debts."

Barnaby pulled out one more document from his pocket and handed it over. It read: *In the event of the death of the recipient of the unpaid loan, all possessions, including property, livestock, and those living under the roof, will belong to the loaner in question.*

The words blurred as her mind spun, especially when she noticed her father's signature yet again on the offending document. "This cannot be legal. You do not own me or my mother."

"Oh, yes, I do," he snarled, snatching the documents back and tucking them on his person. "I came to Millbrook to take what is almost now mine but instead I found you. I tried romancing you, Mirabelle. I showered you with compliments and gifts and promises no one in their right mind would refuse. I do not like taking no for an answer." He stepped closer until he backed her into the trunk of a tree, towering above her. "I legally own you and your mother, even now before your father has died. If you do not marry me, I will send your mother to live in a poor city with nothing but the clothes on her back."

She glared at him. "You wouldn't dare."

"It's not something I take pleasure in doing. But I will."

Her chin wobbled as her resolve wavered. "I am far from nobility. Why would you choose me over anyone else?"

"The wolves love pure bloods, true. But do you know what surpasses generations of pure-blooded nobility?" He ran a hand up her arm and cupped her chin in his hand. "Beauty." He dropped his hand and took a single step backward, allowing her to take a breath into her lungs. "The ranch is mine. The barn is mine. The house is mine. The land is mine. You will marry me. Or you will have nothing."

She spat at his feet. Blindingly fast, he lifted his hand as if to strike her. She flinched away, but the strike never came. Anger seethed from his intoxicated mouth, but he never touched her.

"Gilberd will marry me," she insisted. "And we will not be left wanting."

"If you marry Gilberd, he will go to prison for ten years for stealing my property. Go right ahead. Get him locked up for a decade. He will come to despise you, and you will still be left with nothing."

Mirabelle's chin wobbled as she imagined Gilberd locked behind bars, his future ruined because she'd desperately wanted love. He would resent her for taking away his dreams and his freedom just as he managed to reach them.

No, she couldn't do that to him.

She would never be able to live with herself.

"When?" she asked in a small, defeated voice, which only inspired Barnaby's smug grin to grow wider.

"Two weeks from now in Edilann. The preparations for the wedding are going forward as we speak. All we need to do is show up." He pulled her closer, and her weary soul refused to fight back this time. "I will have full cooperation from you. Understand?"

When she didn't answer, he slipped a ring onto her finger, making her not a fiancée but a possession to be used for his own vile purposes. The weight of the piece of jewelry knocked her off balance until her surroundings spun and her stomach threatened to heave.

"I have business to finalize here." His grin stretched even wider if it were possible. "I will see you soon. Real soon."

And then he mounted his horse and kicked it into a canter, leaving dust in his triumphant wake.

Mirabelle gasped in a breath, which promptly turned into a sob, until tears trailed unceasingly down her face. She wept for herself, for her mother, for her father, and for Gilberd, who she now knew she could never have. She wept for her bleak future.

Because without Gilberd, she would have nothing of value at all.

A week and a half had passed since Gilberd had last seen Mirabelle. By now, he reckoned she'd received his letter, which meant they were officially courting. But now only one problem remained…

How was he supposed to convince her within two weeks to not only marry him, but pack up her life, her family, her livelihood, and join him in Edilann? A quick wedding could happen in Millbrook before they left the town. But he couldn't ignore the monstrosity of a brick settled at the bottom of his stomach, telling him something wasn't quite right.

He inhaled a long breath and let it out slowly to calm himself as he stood at the side of an extravagant ballroom a step behind Prince Sterling. Musicians played a flawless ensemble in the corner of the room. Skirts twirled as wedding guests danced across shiny marble floors beneath the light of an enormous chandelier. Fans and eyelashes fluttered as women gossiped and flirted.

And Sterling?

Well, he stood quietly by his lonesome, taking in the scene with intelligent but cautious eyes. Gilberd couldn't help but notice the boy's attention focusing on a group of girls around his own age, though his expression gave nothing away as he watched them talking and laughing amongst themselves. One girl, in particular, stood out from the rest with lavish clothing, flawless hair, and numerous jewels sparkling around her neck.

"Go ask her to dance," Gilberd urged, but Sterling's eyes widened with terror as he adamantly shook his head and leaned closer to the wall. "Why not?"

The boy wrinkled his nose and shot him a look of disbelief. "She's a girl."

He tipped his head to the side and studied the prince. "I'm trying to figure out whether you think she's pretty or has cooties." But it wasn't disgust in his expression but fear.

"I'm not asking her to dance."

"I know you've had dancing lessons. What are they for if not to dance?"

Sterling narrowed his eyes at him. "If it's so easy, why don't *you* ask someone to frolic about the room with you?"

"Because I'm not allowed when I'm working, for one. I have no clue how to dance, for two. And for three, I have a swain waiting at home. I won't dance with other women."

The prince crossed his arms and frowned, resentment burning in his eyes. It flickered too brightly in his expression to have grown only in the past minute. Something had provoked him. But what? "I hate it here. I want to go home."

Gilberd quirked his mouth to the side as he tried to glean information about Prince Sterling's sudden behavior, shifting from uncomfortable bystander to bitter heir. At ten years old, it wasn't uncommon to have bouts of anger, even before he started growing facial hair. But something about this didn't seem normal for someone his age.

He shifted his attention to the throngs of dancers twirling across the dance floor, particularly honing in on the young girls huddled on the opposite side of the ballroom, giggling and talking excitedly amongst themselves. But when he turned back to Sterling, he was gone.

"Kingdom's glory," he swore as he pushed away from the wall and searched the vicinity for a head of brown hair and a pair of startling blue eyes. However, Sterling was nowhere within view. Not beside his parents as they conversed with other nobility. Not loitering near the refreshment table. But gone.

He silently cursed. Only two days into his new job and he already managed to lose his charge.

Trying not to make a scene of his departure, Gilberd slowly ambled out of the room to avoid notice, and only when he reached the torch-lit hallway did he quicken his pace. He glanced back and forth across the corridor, peeked into the rooms he passed, and he placed his foot on the bottom step of the staircase with the intention to climb when he heard the faintest sniff.

His heart sank to his toes when he thought he recognized the sound.

He turned and followed the source of the second sniff until he found himself standing in the doorway leading outside into the dark gardens, empty aside from the lone figure sitting on a bench overlooking a series of statues within a circle of rose bushes, the boy facing away from him.

For a moment, he debated whether he should do his duty as a guard and maintain his distance or if he should provide the comfort he suspected Sterling never received at home.

Silently, he crossed the space between them and joined him on the bench. Sterling said nothing, but his slumped shoulders and crestfallen expression spoke volumes.

Knowing the prince was not great at starting conversations, Gilberd spoke first. "Do you want to talk about it?"

Sterling shrugged. "I don't want to get married."

He cast a confused, sideways glance at the prince. "You are ten years old. No one's getting married."

Again, the boy shrugged as he dug the toe of his shoe into the dirt. "My father is negotiating an arranged marriage for me."

His brows furrowed as the new information sank in. The king hadn't mentioned anything to him. Although it wasn't necessarily his business, he thought something large enough to affect his young charge was important to know. Clearly, Sterling was unhappy about it, and he highly suspected it was the reason he kept running away.

"You don't like the girl?"

"I don't like *any* girls. Girls are gross."

He was tempted to laugh, but the timing was terrible. "Forgive me for my lack of knowledge. But why are they arranging a marriage so many years before you even come of age?"

"To secure an alliance before someone else does."

The intelligence in Sterling's voice, in his eyes, took him aback. Although he was only a decade old, he clearly was smarter than he let on.

Not only smart, but he was shouldering responsibilities no ten-year-old boy should have to shoulder. But perhaps royalty did things differently, and he couldn't simply brush it off.

"You are a prince, Sterling. And someday you will be a king. I believe securing an alliance is an important thing to do in your position. But also… You are a *prince*. Women will be lining up for a chance to marry you, no matter your age." He paused to fiddle with his sleeve, wondering how much power he had here. Probably very little, but he knew he needed to try anyway. "I think you should have more of a choice in your position. What if I spoke to your parents? If I can't convince them to stop negotiations, maybe I can persuade them to postpone them until you're older."

Sterling straightened and swiped a hand beneath his nose, followed by another sniff. "You would do that?"

Gilberd shrugged. "I can try. I'm just a guard. I'm more likely to get fired than receive an audience with your father."

The prince's mouth clamped shut, his brows furrowed as he stared into his lap. A few long moments of silence passed, and this time he knew he should hold his tongue. He wanted to be Sterling's friend, maybe even confidante, but he also knew his place.

Finally, the boy lifted his head and frowned. "I don't want you to get fired."

"I don't either. But my job is looking out for your well-being. The least I can do is try."

A deep weariness stared back at him from the eyes of a ten-year-old, making the boy look far older than he was. Sterling needed to do boy things like climb trees, throw mud balls, and hit things with sticks. Not just sit in a stuffy room studying all day, every day, reading books and learning things. He needed to play.

But Gilberd might only have so much leeway with the king.

"Just give me two weeks," he said, brushing an imaginary speck of dust off his pants. "I have to get a few things straightened out at home first."

"You will come back, won't you?"

"Of course, I will." He held out his pinky, and Sterling stared at it with a level of hope but caution in his eyes. "I promise I'll come back."

Hesitantly, Sterling hooked his pinky around his and they shook on it. A powerful surge of emotion slammed into him, and he swallowed it back before the prince noticed. Gilberd swore he wouldn't let Sterling down. Ever. Because if no one else was going to be there for him when he needed it, he silently promised to come through himself. No matter what he needed to do to achieve it.

For the first time in her life, everything around Mirabelle felt bleak, without promise. The four walls surrounding her were gray and dusty and suffocating. Her body felt weak and tired. Resentment buzzed in her mind for the father who lay in the other room, coming closer and closer to taking his last breath as he coughed and wheezed and choked on his own spittle.

She hated her father.

She loved her father.

But through all the confusing thoughts and emotions whirling through her head, she knew she must believe he'd had no other choice but to sell his own wife and child to a devious loaner. Surely, he'd thought there was no other direction to turn in such a dire situation.

She must believe it.

Otherwise, she would fall apart entirely.

Someone rapped on the door. But Mirabelle was in no mood to face Barnaby. Not today.

From where she sat at the table, listening to her father's wheezing breaths and her mother's soothing words, she ran her hands through her hair, over her face, and hid her tearful eyes within the darkness of her palms.

Go away, Barnaby, she silently pleaded in her mind. *Not today. Just go away.*

She twirled his ring around her finger, her stomach churning sickly at the weight of it on her hand. Slowly, her hand lowered over the knife resting on the table, and she tightly gripped the handle. If Barnaby wanted a beauty at his side, then he would truly hate having a wife with a scar across her face.

But in the end, she sighed and relinquished her grip on the knife, knowing with or without a scar, she and her mother relied on Barnaby legally and financially. Her mother didn't deserve to live on the streets. She would not survive.

A rap on the door sounded again, and Mirabelle heaved a long sigh as she finally found enough strength to stand, though her legs felt heavy as she crossed the room to the door. She unlocked it and pulled it open, but instead of finding blond hair and blue eyes, she stared back at a pair of brown eyes high enough for her to have to crane her neck.

"Gilberd!" she gasped, and with panicked movements, she slammed the door shut behind her and hid her left hand behind her back to conceal Barnaby's ring. "I wasn't expecting you until tomorrow."

He ran a hand across the back of his neck and regarded her cautiously, and for a moment, she wondered if someone had told him about her recent engagement.

The mere thought of it turned her stomach, and she reached out to the railing to steady herself, her breaths trembling from her lungs.

"Well, someone got sick, which forced us to return a day early and…" He blew out a long breath. "I have a lot of things I need to speak to you about. Is now a good time?"

Mirabelle released another shuddering breath, and she covered her eyes with her hand as she attempted to regain control over her emotions.

Barnaby's words echoed in her mind. *If you marry Gilberd, he will go to prison for ten years for stealing my property.*

The thought of losing Gilberd forever broke her heart. She loved him. Dearly. But putting him in prison just to save herself? However, she knew he was a persistent man. He needed to believe she'd chosen this. Otherwise, she would doom him and his career as a soldier.

It was for the best for him to forget about her. No matter how much it broke her heart. "Actually, there is something I need to say first." She swallowed and slowly lowered her hand from her face, only to witness the deep concern in Gilberd's eyes. "I—"

"Get away from my fiancée!" Barnaby shouted from the edge of the property. He thundered toward them on his black steed, blond hair flying across his forehead, before he hopped down and approached Gilberd with fury painted on his face.

"Excuse me?" Gilberd descended the steps, and Mirabelle watched in horror as he pulled up his sleeves to his elbows. "After everything you've done, you dare to come here and make such a bold claim?" He shoved Barnaby's shoulders, and the man stumbled backward at the mere force behind Gilberd's strength. "I told you I would break all your fingers if you came near Mirabelle again. And that's *after* I smash the teeth out of your mouth."

"You heard me, Spill-wiper." Barnaby shoved him back, but it hardly made a dent in the larger man's sturdy frame. "My *fiancée*. You don't really think I was going to disappear without making her mine?"

The words contorted Gilberd's expression with rage, and Mirabelle inhaled sharply as he drew back his fist and punched Barnaby in the jaw.

He stumbled backward, tripped over a rock, and crashed to the ground. He stood no chance to climb to his own two feet before Gilberd grabbed him by the shirt, lifted him up much to Barnaby's squeaking protests and ripping fabric, and shoved him backward.

But this time, Barnaby caught himself, released a war cry, and slammed his shoulder into Gilberd's ribs.

They traded blows back and forth until Gilberd's superior agility and strength allowed him to get the other man into a headlock, arm pinned behind his back.

"Stop," Mirabelle murmured, hands pressed to her heart.

Neither of them heard her half-hearted plea, and just as Gilberd swung Barnaby around, she yelled it louder. "Stop!"

However, the momentum of the swing sent Barnaby stumbling straight toward a water trough, followed by a resounding *splash* as he fell in, nearly fully submerged.

"Please stop," she sobbed, wishing she didn't have to push through this, wishing she didn't have to witness the way she was about to break Gilberd's heart. She held out her left hand to display the ring and said, "It's true. We are engaged."

Gilberd's entire body froze, his shoulders rigid as he slowly turned to face her until the shock was visible in his disbelieving stare.

His lips parted as his gaze flickered to the ring, then to Barnaby struggling to pull himself out of the trough, and finally when he met her gaze, devastation shattered his expression.

She felt her own heart rip in tandem with his. More than anything, she wanted him in her life. As her husband. As her friend. As the father of her children.

But no option remained but to follow through with the marriage to Barnaby.

"Why?" he asked in a hoarse whisper before shaking his head. "What about your letter? I replied only a week ago. How could you have changed your mind so quickly?"

She blinked rapidly, fighting off the tears threatening to fall. She lowered her voice to keep Barnaby from overhearing and replied with a semi-truth. "We needed the money."

He tenderly cradled his ribs but never broke his stare. "I could have provided for you. I got a good job in Edilann. It's what I wanted to speak to you about." He took a step closer, but unable to bear the agony of his proximity, she stepped back. He paused. "Please, don't go through with the marriage.

I promise you, I will take care of you and your parents. You don't need that loafer's money. *Please*."

Swallowing, she decided lying was the only option to keep him safe, to keep her family safe. "I-I-I care for him. I want to marry him. I don't want to marry you."

His jaw clenched and his eyes hardened. Instead of the heartbreak she expected to find in his expression, she only found determination. "You are a liar," he accused. "And if you won't tell me the truth, then I will find out by myself."

Without another word, he spun around and stormed toward the road but not before glaring in Barnaby's direction. In response, Barnaby lifted his middle finger.

Mirabelle's heart crumbled to the ground at her feet as she watched Gilberd's retreating back. Perhaps she should have told him the truth, that she was trapped in a contract her father had signed, throwing away her future and her freedom in a single pen stroke. But how could she burden him with such knowledge?

The only way she could think of to get out of such a contract was a large sum of money to pay off her father's debts. But even if she sold the cattle, the house, the property, and every single one of her belongings, it wasn't enough. Gilberd, especially, didn't have that kind of money, even with the wage of a soldier.

There was no hope for her, so it was best to shatter Gilberd's hope as well.

The door clicked open behind her, and her mother stared back at her, face as pale as a sheet. No tears marked her face, but the heartbreak in her eyes was enough to tell her what happened.

Her mother swallowed once, and when she spoke, her voice cracked. "Your father has passed."

ilberd left the Waters' property in an angry daze. He kicked a fence post along his way down the road, followed by a pebble, which skipped across the dusty path and settled somewhere in the tall grass.

Mirabelle had accepted Barnaby's proposal? Out of all the people in the world, she chose *him*? He knew she wasn't stupid. Something wasn't right about this situation, and he planned to get to the bottom of it. Wherever it led him.

He stopped short in front of the inn, his brows furrowed when he found a second horse tied to the hitching post next to his. The Edilann crest was emblazoned on the blue and gold saddle blanket, and he scratched his scruffy chin in confusion. Had a guard followed him to Millbrook? Why didn't the king warn him to expect company?

Confusion floated over his head as he entered the inn through the back door. His mother sat at her apothecary table, grinding herbs in a mortar as she spoke to the person sitting with her, a smile on her face.

Short. Brown hair. Blue eyes.

His heart dropped to his toes, horror stretching across his face as he pulled on his hair. "No no no no no! First, I'm going to get fired. Then I'm going to get killed." Both his mother and Sterling stared at him with wide eyes. The infuriating boy at least had the decency to drop his gaze shamefully into his lap. "Sterling, why have you followed me here?"

"Sterling?" His mother's face paled as she snapped her attention to the boy. "The prince?"

He crossed the room in only a few strides. "Do you have an escort? Or did you come by yourself?"

"I switched places with one of the servants!" Sterling protested. "I promise you, no one will notice I'm missing for a few days."

A string of curses escaped on his breath as he gripped his hair with his fingers and slowly turned around as he realized the dangerous situation he now found himself in. He only barely received the position as Sterling's guard, and for the boy to have run away already? Not only that, but he feared the king and queen would think he kidnapped the prince.

"Ma, I need you to write a letter for me. Fast. My life literally depends on how fast the king can get this."

As his mother penned a hasty letter, word for word as he instructed, Sterling's face fell the moment she sealed it in an envelope and addressed it to the palace.

"Please don't tell them where I am," the prince begged. "I don't want to go back home."

Gilberd wasn't sure whether to frown at how he would risk his life rather than be a prince or scold him for attempting such a dangerous feat to begin with. Would no one notice his absence for several days? Truly?

But then he remembered his blind-as-a-bat tutor, and he realized the king and queen didn't make spending time with their son a priority.

Pulling up a chair, he sat at the table with Ma and Sterling, heaving a sigh. Perhaps this excursion would be good for the prince. To get away from the palace. To meet his subjects and witness how they lived life.

The king made him Sterling's bodyguard for a reason, instructing him to follow him at all times, even if he should run away. Only, he never expected it to happen so soon.

He pushed a second paper toward his mother and asked her to redraft the letter. This time, he informed the king Sterling followed him to Millbrook without his knowledge, but he promised to protect him with his life and bring him back safely when he returned to the castle in a week and a half.

Although he feared the king would fire him for this, the man was level-headed and knew Sterling had a tendency to run away. Would Gilberd face consequences? Or would the king allow Sterling much-needed space to clear his head?

There was only one way to find out.

After taking the letter from his mother, he stood, and Sterling stood with him as if determined to follow. He tied his sword back onto his belt from where he'd left it by the door. It wasn't going to leave his side anytime soon when he had a charge to protect.

"Are there any rooms available?" he asked his mother.

She winced and shook her head. "We're completely full, what with several events happening in Edilann lately. But we should clear out a little in a few days." She curtsied. "Forgive me, Your Highness."

He couldn't leave Sterling's side, so he asked, "Can you lay out a bed roll in my room? I'll sleep on the floor." He almost laughed at the absurdity of the situation. Sharing a room with the future king of Edilann? Guarding him and keeping him safe?

He'd never imagined himself in such a situation.

When she nodded, he started for the back door. Sure enough, Sterling followed him, a sense of eagerness in his step. Thankfully, he'd already explained his new position to his mother. Only, he'd never expected to introduce them in his lifetime.

"Can you just…" Sterling stuffed his hands into his pockets and stared at the ground as they made their way through town. "Not tell my father at all?"

"And then what?" Mr. Galloway's pig squealed as they passed the older man's house, and Gilberd rolled his eyes. The man really needed to fix his fence. Perhaps he would do it himself. "The king will send soldiers to find you, and one of the first places they will look is here."

A hefty sigh escaped the boy's lungs. "I only thought…you of all people might understand."

He stopped in front of the orchard where he'd kissed Mirabelle, and his heart tumbled out of his ribcage, splatting to the ground as heartache shoved its way into the hole in his chest. He refused to allow her to go through with this wedding. Surely, she didn't truly mean it when she said she didn't want to marry him.

A shuddering breath left his lips as he tried to push her from his thoughts when he needed to focus on this situation first. "I do understand," he said quietly, now facing him. "I'm sure your lack of freedom is frustrating to you."

Sterling nodded and dug his toe into the dirt. "I'm tired of everyone telling me what to do. I'm done being a prince. I don't want to do it anymore."

The boy's hysterics drew attention from passersby, and some of the townsfolk he'd known since he was a child looked from him, to Sterling, and back to him before speaking in gossiping whispers. He doubted any of them knew what their sovereign prince looked like. Therefore, people were bound to speculate on how the two of them might be acquainted or even related. They had a similar shade of brown hair, but that's where the resemblance ended. Besides, they were fifteen years apart. Sterling was too old for anyone to possibly believe Gilberd was his father, but a cousin or nephew wasn't out of the question.

Gilberd placed a hand on Sterling's shoulder and almost retracted it when he realized *who* he was touching. But the emotion clouding the boy's eyes kept him from removing it, as if he needed a strong, reassuring presence in his life.

"For a week and a half, you don't have to be a prince. Everything will be fine." He squeezed his shoulder before dropping his hand. "Besides, you'll get a taste of the small-town life. It's not as glamorous as you might think."

Sterling's mouth twitched as if he tried not to smile, and they fell into step once more as they crossed the dusty street and dropped the letter off at the post office, which would leave for Edilann in an hour. A part of him felt like he should deliver the letter himself with Sterling in tow but...

...Mirabelle.

He pinched the bridge of his nose and took several deep breaths to steady himself. He needed answers. What had happened in the short time of his absence? Who could he ask?

Well, for starters, he would seek out his mother first. As an innkeeper, she and his father practically ran the gossip mill, second only to the tavern during midnight hours.

He returned to the inn, and as he passed Barnaby's room, he flipped off the door, his nostrils flaring with a bout of anger. He was *this* close to hiding poison ivy in the man's bed. However, he didn't dare when his parents' reputation was in danger.

He found both his mother and father bustling about his room, changing sheets, fluffing pillows, and placing a vase of flowers on a table beside the window. When they entered, each bowed to Sterling, his father dipping at the waist several times.

"Your Highness," his father said, bowing yet again, "I am humbled by your presence at our inn. Camilla is bringing up supper as we speak, and Jeremy is brushing down your horse in the stables. Please, if there is anything we can do for you here, do not hesitate to ask."

Sterling glanced toward Gilberd as if unsure how to proceed in such a situation. But manners lessons must have kicked in because he dipped his head in acknowledgement while nervously shuffling his feet.

"Thank you," he replied in a small voice.

When his father approached to pepper Sterling with questions about how he liked this or that, Gilberd grasped his mother's elbow and pulled her into the hallway, out of earshot of the other two.

"Gil, what—"

"Why is Mirabelle engaged to that blockhead?" His voice cracked, and he took a moment to breathe deeply to center his emotions. "She said she would wait for me. Why, after a week and a half, has she turned back on her promise?"

His mother's brows furrowed, and the corners of her mouth turned downward. "I didn't know she accepted Barnaby's proposal." She rubbed her hand up and down his arm as a comforting gesture. "I wonder if it's because her father just passed."

The pulse fluttering in his veins stumbled at the revelation, and his open mouth slowly closed until his expression fell with the heartache Mirabelle must be feeling.

"I didn't know. When did he pass?"

"An hour ago, I believe."

He sighed and leaned heavily against the wall, rubbing the ache in his temple with his fingers. "And there I was, making it worse for her by picking a fight with Barnaby. I didn't know." He groaned. "I am such an idiot."

In the moment, he had been nervous but happy to see her. But now? He recalled her red, puffy eyes, the way she'd hidden her hand behind her back, the exhaustion in her shoulders as if she simply could carry no more burdens.

"What am I supposed to do?" he asked quietly. "Was I wrong to assume she returned my feelings?" His voice caught again, and he closed his eyes to fight against his wavering emotions.

"I promise you, Gilberd." His mother ran her hand up and down his arm again as if trying to stir some warmth into his frigid veins. "She loves you. When she received your letter, she was absolutely, purely relieved."

"When did she receive it?"

"Three days ago."

147

Another long sigh left his lungs as he opened his eyes and stared at the wooden wall before him, a section scarred from moving furniture. "Is she unhappy about me becoming Sterling's guard?"

She shook her head. "She doesn't know. She thinks you accepted a position as a soldier. But she was *happy*."

"Then something happened within the last three days to push her into accepting Barnaby's suit."

"It would seem so." She paused to glance into the room where his father continued his groveling while Sterling shuffled his feet with immense discomfort in his eyes. "Have you asked her?"

He nodded. "She lied to my face." He pressed his lips together. "Do you have a key to Barnaby's room?"

His mother gave him a stern look, and he shied away from the idea altogether. "You know very well I will never give it to you. I stand by a strict privacy policy for our guests." She frowned. "No matter who they are or what they have done."

Frustration clawed at him as he realized the hopelessness of his circumstances. He'd been hoping to run off to Edilann with a new wife by the end of the week, not lose his spot to someone else.

But he forced himself to take a deep breath. This wasn't about him. No matter how angry or frustrated he was, this was about her. She was hurting. And he hoped to take away a fraction of her ache in any way he could.

"Your Highness," he said, addressing Sterling with a slight bow of his head, "I have an errand—"

"I'm coming," he gasped, relief shooting through his expression as he rushed toward the door. For someone who didn't want princely attention for a week and a half, he was doing a poor job of avoiding it. Not as if he had much choice in the matter anyway.

"It's a…personal matter."

"I'll stay back a bit."

Who was he to deny the prince of Edilann? "Very well."

A numbness took a hold of Mirabelle's heart and slithered through her veins as she and her mother made preparations for Papa's funeral taking place tomorrow. Quickly. Quietly. Accepting help from neighbors when offered and politely turning those away who demanded too much.

But someone who didn't offer to help?

Barnaby.

Rather, he was impatient to whisk her away to Edilann and force her to the altar.

Mama tucked the white scarf she'd knitted around her father's body, and together, with the help of the priestess, they blessed his spirit and closed the lid of the coffin, nailing it together with a heartbreaking finality.

The priestess drew two overlapping triangles on top of the coffin with ink, the symbol of the Mother Goddess, to guide him into the afterlife. And when she finished the prayer, she offered them a regretful look.

"I'm sorry that there is not currently a grave dug in the churchyard. Either you can pay for someone to dig it or find someone to do it before tomorrow afternoon."

Knowing they hadn't the money for such an expenditure, and she feared owing Barnaby anything else, she nodded her head. "We'll take care of it ourselves."

With a final farewell, the holy woman exited their home, leaving behind a gap of silence Mirabelle had no idea how to fill. She'd expected this day to come for many weeks. But now that it was here? It was as if a chunk of her heart was missing, a chunk of her life. Because her father was gone. And the gap didn't feel right.

Several minutes later, someone knocked on the door. It could have been a neighbor or someone from town. But she recognized the knock, hesitant yet strong, and her entire being longed to throw it open and jump into the man's arms. But the weight on her finger held her back.

Slowly, she opened the door to find Gilberd on her porch and a familiar-looking boy with brown hair chasing the chickens across the yard. But instead of an accusatory look, Gilberd held a bouquet of wildflowers in his hand.

"I'm so sorry," he murmured, eyes heavy with sadness to mirror her own. "Your father was a good man."

A shuddering breath escaped her as she nodded. "Yes, he was." She had to believe it.

"What can I do for you, Mira?" he asked quietly. To her dismay, she noticed him keeping his distance when he didn't reach out but continued to keep several paces between them. "What do you need?

So many things.

Oh, how she longed to tell him the truth. How she longed to feel his strong arms around her, keeping her afloat when her world was crumbling to pieces around her. Which was why she despised herself for saying, "Gilberd, you need to leave."

For several long moments, he stared back at her, not saying a single word as he searched her eyes. But then he backed up several steps and placed the bouquet of flowers on the wooden porch railing.

"You shouldn't have to go through this alone. If you need me—"

"I'm not alone. My mother and Barnaby are my support now."

Gilberd raised his arms and gestured to the ranch in one grand sweep. "Where is he, then? Hmm? Where is your fiancé? Why is he not here with you in your time of need?"

Instead of arguing, the dam behind her eyes broke and a gush of tears trailed down her cheeks and over her chin. She was tired. So very tired.

"Forgive me." He reached out to the railing and hung his head. "I didn't come here to make this worse. I wanted to offer *something*. Anything you will allow me to give you." When she didn't answer, heartbreaking vulnerability stared back at her. "Is it me? Did I do something? Did I say something? I know this is terrible timing, Mira, but surely you understand why I can't wait."

He was too persistent. She hated him for it. She loved him for it.

"You're right. This is terrible timing." And she hated herself for hurting the man she loved.

Instead of probing further, he asked, "When is the funeral?"

"Tomorrow at noon."

For a moment, he seemed as if he might reach out and pull her against him, crushing him against his chest in a fierce embrace. But he didn't. Because he couldn't. Perhaps they should have eloped while they still innocently could. It was too late now.

"My family will be there. Like I said, your father was a good man. We all loved him. We all love your family."

The meaning of his words sank deep into her soul. Although he didn't directly tell her he loved her, she knew he meant it that way from his soft, intentful gaze. She closed her eyes, afraid to witness his love and also scared he might see the truth of her love himself.

When she opened her eyes, he and the boy were gone.

S omeone in mourning should never have to dig a grave, Mirabelle decided.

Her aching fingers clenched around the wooden handle of a shovel. Blisters sprouted on her palms despite the leather gloves she wore. Dirt clung to the bottom of her dress and somehow shook free from her hair.

The funeral was in an hour, and she was only halfway done.

The rich scent of earth permeated her nostrils as she continued to dig, all while her mother apologized profusely for not being able to help when her tremors were so terrible. But with one more toss of dirt, she once more appeased her guilt with a few words of comfort.

A trickle of blood dripped from the edge of one of her gloves and down her wrist as if one of her blisters popped. She ignored the pain and thrust the metal end of the shovel into the dirt. But before she could convince her throbbing arms to throw out another mound, someone's hand shot out and grasped the shovel, preventing her from continuing.

She glanced up from her place in the soft earth and met a pair of soft brown eyes filled with sympathy and love. Tears blurred Gilberd's image as he helped her out of the hole with a strong hand, and before she managed a protest, he guided her to the bench beside her mother and took up the task of digging the grave himself.

The same boy from yesterday picked up another shovel and hopped inside the hole as well. But no matter how many tears of gratitude she wiped away, they continued to spill down her cheeks and distort their two images.

She'd seen the boy before. But where? From small glimpses, she'd noticed his finer clothing, his messy hair, and his bright blue eyes. But no matter how hard she tried, she couldn't place how she knew him.

One by one, guests began arriving in the churchyard, standing around her and her mother while offering their condolences. A spark of irritation burned in her belly when she noticed Barnaby was absent, but it burned out just as quickly when she realized she didn't care. She didn't want him there.

Which was why the spark returned with a vengeance when he rounded the corner, whistling with his hands in his pockets as if today was a celebration rather than a day to mourn.

"Have you no ounce of sympathy in your body?" Mirabelle hissed when he approached, glaring at the horrid man. "I am burying my father today."

"Of course." His mouth turned downward into a mock pout, and perhaps if she were a lady of court, she might have believed his performance. "I hate seeing you so distraught. It breaks my heart to pieces."

If only you had a heart.

In a sudden launch, the boy flew out of the grave and stumbled on his feet as if not quite ready for the momentum of what she assumed was Gilberd tossing him out of the hole. With the help of two other men, Gilberd climbed out of the hole next and immediately retrieved his sword, tying it to his belt.

She watched the way he moved with confidence, the way his muscles flexed as he handled the weapon, the way he towered above most other people but still possessed an heir of kindness behind his strength.

As if feeling her gaze on him, he turned and met her eye for the briefest second. But the moment was shattered as Barnaby gasped suddenly and bent halfway into a bow. "Your Highness!"

Her eyes shot open in shock as several others around her exclaimed their surprise and bowed and curtsied in tandem. She hastened to her feet, searching for the king. But then she noticed they were all bowing to the young boy, who always spent time with Gilberd.

The boy...

The *prince*.

She remembered him now. She'd seen him only once at a jousting tournament in Edilann two years back.

She hastily dipped into a curtsy, wondering why he was in Millbrook of all places. At her father's *funeral*.

"Your Highness," Barnaby said again, adopting a charming smile for the prince as he took several steps forward. But then another round of gasps filled the churchyard as Gilberd stepped forward and drew his sword.

Gilberd held his sword out to the side, using it as a barrier between Barna-idiot and Sterling, whose clothing was spotted with dirt from helping him dig the grave. He adopted a serious expression to let the aristocrat know it was not a good idea to advance any farther.

"Prince Sterling did not give you permission to approach." Thankfully, it was directly in his job description to keep others from getting too close unless allowed by the prince, even by the tip of a sword. Within reason, of course.

Barnaby's mouth opened, closed, and opened again as if struggling for words, his expression as confused as the rest of the people surrounding them. "But what…?" He glanced between the two of them and addressed the prince. "What are you doing with a lowly innkeeper?"

"He's my new bodyguard," Sterling said with a coldness in his eyes Gilberd hadn't witnessed before. More gasps, and he felt dozens of eyes swivel in his direction, including Mirabelle's astonished gaze. "He saved my life from three assassins."

He briefly wondered if the prince hated the man as much as he did, or if he hated him *because* he did. But the disdain in his tone was unmistakable.

The prince nodded to the ground. "On your knee."

Hastily, Barnaby dropped to one knee with his head bowed in fealty, and only then did Gilberd return his sword to his sheath. Despite his hatred for the man, he was on duty, and therefore, he needed to remain professional and do his job.

A sheen of perspiration dotted Barnaby's forehead, an anxious flicker in his eyes. What did he think the prince was going to do? Hang him?

For everyone's sake, even Barnaby's, he hoped Sterling didn't possess such power even at his young age.

The faintest glimmer of satisfaction washed over him when he glanced at his sovereign prince from the corner of his eye. Sterling was a quiet and withdrawn boy. This was new for him, and it was a good thing.

But as if his courage flickered out, Sterling's mouth clamped shut, and he visibly withdrew before his eyes. It couldn't be easy having the entire kingdom watching him, to never escape scrutiny no matter how far he traveled.

Gilberd stepped in, taking the attention away from Sterling for a few moments. "We came to lay a good man to rest. I think we should get back to it."

Murmurs of agreement made their rounds among the crowd, and thankfully, everyone settled down while the priestess started her funeral sermon. He dared to glance toward Mirabelle, afraid of her reaction. But when she mouthed, *Thank you*, his heart settled a fraction. What seemed like a hundred questions lay within her eyes, but then they glanced away from each other to focus on the sermon.

When it finished, Gilberd, and several other men, helped lower the coffin into the ground using ropes, and surprisingly, Sterling helped heave the slack ropes back up. The guests each tossed flowers onto the coffin before covering it once more with the dirt, followed by a gravestone.

The finality of saying goodbye to Mr. Waters stole the breath from his lungs. But then the sound of weeping brought his attention to Mirabelle, who covered her eyes with her hands as tears leaked through her fingers and down her chin. His heart broke for her and for himself, especially when Barnaby wrapped an arm around her shoulders and pulled her into his side.

He quickly turned away from the scene and stuffed his hands into his pockets. More than anything, he wanted to comfort Mirabelle, to pull her into his arms, to kiss her tears away...

But instead, he walked at a brisk pace toward the road, his lungs heaving with each breath, and he didn't stop until his shaking legs could no longer hold his weight. He only made it to the edge of his parents' property when his legs gave out. He collapsed onto a bench beneath a tree, head in his hands.

Each breath shuddered from his lungs as he realized just how much he'd lost. Mirabelle. His lovely Mirabelle.

The bench creaked beside him, and he rubbed his hand along his face to try to calm himself down. "I just need a minute."

"She pushed him away," Sterling said quietly.

"Huh?" Gilberd lifted his head and glanced toward the boy, who tapped his feet against the ground as he stared at his shoes.

"The woman you kept looking at. She pushed the man away."

The revelation should have calmed his frazzled nerves, but it did nothing to soothe the ache. "She is still wearing his ring. It doesn't matter." He stood quickly before he could fully break down in front of his charge. "I'm going to start packing my belongings. I think it's best if we return to Edilann soon." And then he remembered his station at the last moment as he bowed his head. "With your permission, Your Highness."

The prince nodded mutely and didn't argue against returning, but the careful and intelligent way Sterling watched him formed a pit of uneasiness in his stomach. What could Gilberd even do about the situation? If Mirabelle wanted to marry Barnaby, especially after all the sweet moments they'd shared, then what more could he do?

Nothing. Because perhaps Mirabelle never loved him to begin with.

14

*D*earest Mirabelle,

Gilberd's eyes smarted, his hands shaking as he struggled to write the words on the parchment. Not only was forming the words difficult with his lack of literacy, but saying goodbye tightened his gut and filled him with emotions he'd never felt before. Longing. Regret. Heartache. Love.

With a deep breath, he continued his shaky words.

This letter has no place in your life. Not anymore. But I couldn't leave without saying something, and I apologize, but I cannot say these words to your face. I need a clean break, and then… I suppose we might see each other during special events at the palace, but we will be vastly different ranks at that point.

I wanted you to know how much I love and adore you. You are beautiful, smart, you make me laugh, you make me want to shout your name from the peak of the eastern mountains. You were the light in my life. My light, my joy, my heart. I only wish I could have been enough for you. You deserve the world, and I truly wish you every happiness.

-Gilberd

Too late, he realized he spelled at least ten words wrong, and a few of the words were hardly legible. But it had to be enough because it was all he could do.

He glanced side by side at the two letters he'd drafted. One said goodbye, wishing her the best. The other bore his heart and soul out to her, saying if she loved him, if she wanted a life with him as much as he wanted one with her, for her to meet him in Edilann.

He didn't know which letter to leave behind yet. And it terrified him.

After blotting the letters, he sealed each inside its own envelope and tucked them inside his pocket. He stood, but the movement attracted Sterling's attention from where he was attempting to tie the laces on his shoes. Gilberd almost laughed at his failed attempts as he realized a valet likely took care of his laces. If the boy truly wanted to run away from home, he was far from ready to make it on his own.

"Are you going to see that girl?" Sterling asked.

He shook his head. "I'm going to drop by her house, and I'll be back." He nodded toward the window, down below at the guards now stationed outside the inn, sent by the king himself. The man hadn't ordered Gilberd to bring his son back home. Rather, he'd expressed hope that Sterling could find what he needed in Millbrook.

And that was it. Nothing more.

"She and her mother are gone to the market, so I need to be quick."

"Why not talk to her in person?"

He'd tried that. Several times. "You will understand when you're older, Your Highness." He bowed his head and cleared his throat. "We will depart in an hour for Edilann."

The mention of the city inspired a glum look to cross over his face. Gilberd only wished they could stay in Millbrook for longer, if only to give the boy much-needed freedom. But he couldn't stay even a minute longer than necessary, because if he did, his heart would shatter into a thousand irreparable pieces. He barely kept himself intact as it was.

Making sure for the dozenth time that Sterling was safe, he set off toward the Waters' home while constantly glancing over his shoulder. He wanted to avoid running into Mirabelle, but especially Barn-yard.

A quiet stillness echoed over the landscape as he stepped foot onto the property. It felt like...death. And only then did he realize all the cattle were gone. The vast fields of rippling green grass were empty, void of lowing cows and clanging bells. The gates were wide open and lay still just like the rest of the land.

The orange tabby on the railing stretched as he approached the house and rubbed its face against one of the wooden posts on the porch, uncaring that the world around it was falling apart.

Raising a hand, Gilberd knocked on the door and waited. No sound came within the house, nor did anyone move in his direction. Only then did he dare open the door and enter the threshold.

A breath stuttered from his lungs to find much of the house bare of belongings. The only things that remained were a dusty sofa, a brown, ratty rug, and the scarred, wooden table he and his friends had eaten around when they'd gathered to work on the Waters' land.

He ran his fingers across the table, remembering a time when the wood had glowed with vibrant life, surrounded by a family with happy smiles.

He ventured farther into the house and peeked inside two separate rooms. One of the rooms held a bed big enough for two, so he passed it and entered the second room. It held a smaller bed tucked into the corner, an armoire in another corner, a circular rug filled with vibrant reds, blues, and greens, and a bedside table stacked with books and papers.

Unable to help himself, he smiled as he ran his fingers over the spines of the books. During their short courtship, Mirabelle had spoken of her love of books and learning, and especially how much she'd loved going to school.

A red spine caught his attention, and he pulled it out to find difficult words staring back at him. His head hurt too much to decipher them, but he thought the title mentioned something about mathematics.

A smaller book thumped to the side as it fell out of place, and Gilberd reached for it with the intent to put it back. But then his heart gave a start when he recognized his name on the front cover.

"What in the..."

He opened to the first page, and although it took a while, he managed to sound out the words. *This book is dedicated to how much I despise Gilberd Keats.*

Ice crawled through his blood as he sat back on his heels, shocked at his new discovery. And like anyone who found a book dedicated to how much someone disliked them, he opened it and started reading.

One page turned into two, which turned into three until a piece of his heart broke off his soul with each page he turned.

Throughout the years, Mirabelle had documented every single thing he'd done to make her life miserable, things he'd done in the name of getting her attention, some of them he'd even considered flirting at the time.

The final piece of his heart fell to the floor and shattered until he knelt in a pool of shards.

Now he knew.

Mirabelle hated him. He'd never stood a chance. Not with his long history of offenses. Why had he ever thought he could court her? Marry her? Start a life with her?

He couldn't because he was a beast. And Mirabelle deserved to be treated like a princess.

A numbness slithered through his blood, his mind, his empty chest as he pulled the farewell letter out of his pocket and placed it on top of the diary on the bed. He spotted a piece of charcoal on the bedside table and penned only six letters on top of the envelope.

Sorry.

He didn't know what else to say when he knew she deserved so much more. He swore to himself he would make up for this. It was too late with Mirabelle. But he would dedicate the rest of his life to protecting Sterling.

With a heavy heart, Gilberd exited the house and shut the door firmly behind himself. He didn't deserve her. He never had.

He only wished he hadn't hurt her so badly.

15

The emptiness of returning home momentarily created a wave of unfamiliar shock shooting up Mirabelle's spine.

She paused in the threshold with her mother at her side as her gaze swept across what used to be a happy place.

In preparation for their move to Edilann, they'd sold what they couldn't bring.

She ran her fingers across Papa's table, recalling Barnaby's reaction to one of the last things remaining of her father. He'd scoffed. *"No one would buy such an ugly piece of furniture. We'll burn it. Or leave the next owners of the house to do the deed themselves."*

"It's not ugly," she whispered to herself. "It's beautiful." Because her father had made it with his own two hands.

"I need to rest," Mama said with a hand held to her head.

"Are you feeling unwell?"

"Just a headache. It's been a…long week."

Mirabelle squeezed her mother's hand as the only gesture of comfort she could offer before the other woman closed herself in her bedroom. The house suddenly felt too quiet, especially with the absence of lowing cattle filling the silence.

Oh, how she longed for love and laughter and the pattering feet of small children running across the floor, for chaos and happiness so full it would nearly burst her heart.

She ventured toward her own room and sighed at finding it nearly bare. Although she'd never owned many things to begin with, it had hurt to part with a few of her treasured belongings.

Her eyebrows furrowed in confusion when she spotted something lying on top of her bed. Only one word was written on the envelope, but it perplexed her even more.

Sorry.

Now, who could have left such a thing? A neighbor expressing their condolences over Papa's death?

She picked up the envelope but almost dropped it as she gasped. Her diary from years ago rested beneath it, one of the bookmarks in a different place than she remembered, making it clear someone had read it.

"No!" she gasped as she tore open the envelope to find Gilberd's words hastily and messily scrawled across the letter. "No, no, no!"

An icy dread crawled through her blood as she quickly read his words, and her heart broke more and more with each sentence. Though, she was surprised there was something left of her heart to break after this past week.

Mirabelle had wanted to kill Gilberd's hope for a future for them. But not like this. This was cruel. Unjust. And her feelings for him were not reflected in the bemoaning of a young girl. The reason they couldn't be together was not his fault. But her diary was enough to incriminate her.

She stuffed the heartbreaking letter into her pocket, rushed out of the room, and slammed the front door of the house behind her. She raced across spongy dirt and soft grass until she threw the barn doors open and snatched a bridle from the wall.

Her father's horse nickered at her when she opened the door to his stable and stepped onto a stool. With a careful, steady hand, she guided the bit into the horse's mouth and buckled the straps around his head. She wasn't sure if she could lift the saddle by herself nor was she sure she could risk spending the extra time trying.

Using the stool to give her more height, she struggled onto the bare back of the horse, hearing a *rrriiippp* in her skirts when she rode astride. But she didn't care. All that mattered was reaching Gilberd. And soon. Because she had a feeling that if she didn't hurry, she might be too late.

"Yah!" she shouted as she kicked the horse's flanks, and it took all the muscle control in her legs just to hold on rather than get thrown off the creature. But once the creature's gait transitioned from a trot to a gallop, the smooth movement made it easier to hold on.

She thundered down the road, kicking up dirt in her wake, first stopping at the inn. Jeremy's wife, Camilla, stood outside, beating the dirt from several rugs with her daughters. As if noticing the urgency in her eyes, the woman pointed toward the road leading out of Millbrook.

"He's gone. He left an hour ago."

"Thank you," she breathed before reining her horse in the direction of the road. She alternated between a walk and a gallop to give the horse intervals of rest, but when she still didn't find Gilberd on the road, despair shook through her core.

Of course, she could travel to Edilann herself, but she was not packed nor outfitted for such a journey. On the road by her lonesome, especially as a woman in the dark, would put her in immense danger.

Hope alighted in her heart when she spotted a rider farther ahead, and she spurred her mount forward. But the hope fell when a weathered old man nodded his head in greeting. Again, she kicked her horse's flanks, the wind whipping through her hair and tearing it from its pins as she renewed her speed. Dusk settled into the sky, deepening the shadows around her. If she didn't find Gilberd within the next half an hour, she would be forced to turn back around and give up her journey.

By then, Barnaby might have already forced her to the altar. Gilberd needed to know the truth before then. He needed to know he wasn't to blame.

A sob of frustration caught in her throat when she passed several other people, but none were the man she was searching for. Could he have taken another road to Edilann? Especially with the prince in tow? Could they have stopped in another town to wait out the night? Were they traveling to Edilann at all?

The sun descended further until the way ahead was far too shadowed for her to spot the dips in the road. She slowed her horse to a walk to avoid the chance of hurting him.

It was too late…

If she'd only told him the truth from the beginning rather than skirting around the situation with lies. If she'd only expressed how much she loved him, if only just once.

But now she would never get the chance.

Mirabelle held a fist to her aching head. This week had been the worst week she'd ever lived. Frustration and heartache tumbled in her chest. She should have thrown that diary out weeks ago. She should have burned it and watched as it turned to ashes. Because now all Gilberd would receive from her was a heartfelt letter *after* she was a married woman.

It wasn't right. This entire situation wasn't right.

A horse snorted on the path ahead, and her head jerked up to find a group of four men on horseback clomping out of the trees and joining the road headed toward Edilann. Her heart soared when she recognized the large, muscled frame of one of the men and the small silhouette of a boy riding beside him.

Pulse now in a frenzy, she kicked her horse into a gallop, garnering the attention of all four of them as they craned their necks to look her way. Gilberd's eyes flashed with surprised recognition moments before she reined her horse to a stop in front of his, blocking his path.

For several long seconds, they stared back at each other. But then the shock in his eyes transitioned into something far too somber for her tastes.

"You read my diary," she accused in a heavy breath.

He pressed his lips together and stared at his hands tightly gripping his horse's reins. He reached into his pocket and waved a letter in the air.

"I meant to drop this off while you were gone. I didn't mean to find it." He paused but never glanced her way. "It had my name on it. Of course, I read it."

A tense silence filled the air as she looked back and forth between him and the letter in his hand. It looked similar to the one she'd found on her bed. But she suspected she'd like what he wrote in this one much more than the heartbreaking words he'd left her to find.

"I hated you, Gilberd Keats. You were the bane of my existence. You were too much for me."

He swallowed and continued to avert his gaze. "I know that now. I never deserved you. I'm sorry."

Ever since he'd returned from Edilann, he hadn't been the same, and she knew it was mostly her fault. If she'd only been honest from the beginning, then perhaps he wouldn't have carried so much unhappiness in his expression, so much burden in his heart.

She kicked her mount forward enough to startle his horse into movement, which forced him to lift his head and rein the creature back into line. Finally, he met her gaze.

Determination locked in her eyes, and she knew she needed to convey the truth. Just once. Because she might never get another opportunity. "But then I got to know you all over again," she continued while holding a hand to her heart to express her sincerity. "You were gentle. Kind. Funny. Selfless. And I questioned if I ever knew you to begin with. Forget what the diary of a young girl said. Listen to the words of the woman I have become. I love you, Gil. With every fiber of my heart."

His eyelids fluttered closed, the hand with the letter drooping to his side. "Then why are you marrying Barnaby?"

"Do you think I have a choice?" she whispered, glancing over his shoulder at Prince Sterling riding his own horse behind him with two more soldiers flanking them. The boy glanced away but it was clear he was listening to their every word.

She ran her fingers through her hair and hugged herself around the torso. "My father buried us in debt. You don't understand, Gil. He *buried* us. No matter how much money you make as a royal guard, you will never earn enough to pay it back. I can sell everything I own *and* add your wage into the mix, and it still isn't enough. Twenty years of loans and interest has stripped me of my freedom." She wiped a hand over her blurry eyes. "I belong to Barnaby by law. We can never have a future together because you will wind up in prison. Do you understand?"

Gilberd stared at her with a slack jaw moments before it snapped shut, followed by fists clenched tight in a ball. "You *what*?" He ran a hand over his face as anger blazed in his eyes, as if finally understanding everything she'd hidden from him up to this point. "You don't belong to *anyone!* How dare he think he can strap you into a marriage like a donkey hauling straw."

She lowered her voice further, not wanting the prince to overhear this next part. "I'm scared, Gil. Barnaby told me he was going to discreetly *pass me around* the upper class to gain favors from other nobles." She swiped at her eyes again, astounded at how much she had cried over the past few days. "You are delusional if you think a marriage to him is something I ever wanted."

When she cleared her vision, she inhaled sharply at the quiet rage brewing in his eyes, like thunder crackling across a midnight sky.

"Take that ring off," he ordered. "I don't care how much debt it is. I will buy it, shoulder it, work five jobs. I don't care. He will never lay his hands on you."

She blinked rapidly. "I signed a contract."

"For what, exactly?"

"To transfer my father's debt to my name to keep me and my mother from going to prison. He owns me."

"Debt slavery is illegal in Edilann," Sterling cut in, causing her to jump at the sound of his voice. "If the debt is transferred to another family member, usually a third party must get involved to negotiate terms. Have you met with a third party?"

"No." She shook her head. "I'm afraid I am not familiar with the more intricate Edilann laws, Your Highness."

However, for the first time in days, hope stirred within her. There had to be another way!

Sterling pulled back on his reins and turned his horse around to face the road leading to Millbrook rather than Edilann. The horse snorted excitedly as if matching the eagerness in the prince's expression.

"I would like to see the contracts myself," Prince Sterling said, sounding far older than a ten-year-old boy. "Either your father was terrible with money. Or..." He glanced over his shoulder and gave her a shy smile. "Or the numbers are wrong."

She and Gilberd shared a look of hope, of love, and he reached across the space between them and took her hand and squeezed. His touch was gentle and filled with the strength of a sturdy rock. *Her* sturdy rock. Why had she ever thought she could face this burden alone? Why had she thought she could keep this from Gilberd? To allow him to think she didn't care for him rather than tell him the entire truth?

"Forgive me for lying to you," she murmured.

"Well..." He shrugged. "The lies didn't hurt too badly because I saw right through you. At least until I didn't."

Hating every breath of space between them, she pulled him closer with the intent of kissing him, but he dipped his chin instead until their foreheads came together in a gentle, intimate touch.

"I'm not yours to kiss, love," he whispered. "Not yet."

"I hate that so much."

"So do I."

After a moment, they parted with a longing glance before spurring their horses forward to follow the prince. She watched Gilberd's strong, confident back as he took up his position of protection for the young boy, the action like second nature. The tale seemed incredulous. Defeating three assassins and taking on the role of a royal bodyguard?

There was only one prince, and she longed to hear the tale of how it happened. But she knew Gilberd was special. She was surprised, yes, but not disbelieving that he managed to find himself in such an important role.

Her heart gave a start when the corner of parchment scraped against her arm, and she glanced down to find Gilberd's envelope tucked beneath her knee, between her leg and the horse's bare back.

She glanced at him, but his focus remained on the road ahead of them.

Carefully, she broke the seal and slid the letter out. Her smile grew more and more with each word she read beneath the waning light, finding his misspelled words endearing and the bearing of his heart and soul swoonworthy. The breath escaped her in a rush at how he expressed his love and admiration for her, and knowing how long it must have taken him to write this, she loved it even more.

If you feel a fraction of what I do, meet me in Edilann. Let's get married.

She held the letter to her heart, her entire soul trembling from such a bold declaration. When Gilberd glanced at her over his shoulder, she mouthed, *I feel more than just a fraction.*

Although she wasn't sure if he understood her silent words, he smiled warmly before returning his attention to the path ahead.

The closer they came to Millbrook, the faster her heart beat with nervous anticipation. Involving the prince himself in her troubles was no small matter. She feared Barnaby would punish her for this if the numbers added up and he still owned her.

By the time they entered the small town, her head spun with a mixture of terror and hope. She refused to give into Barnaby's whims without fighting for the man she loved. At least not anymore. And if she suffered for this in the end, then so be it.

After securing their horses to the hitching post outside the inn and giving them a bucket of oats to fight over in the darkness of night, they stepped foot inside the establishment where Sterling proceeded to order everyone out of the dining room. Those within the vicinity scrambled away until a strange silence filled the space. Not even Gilberd's father dared to enter with refreshments.

Sterling ordered his two soldiers to track down Barnaby, who they found upstairs in his room. He descended the stairs, hastily buttoning his shirt and tucking it inside his pants.

"What is the meaning of this?" Barnaby growled, looking between each of them with a scowl on his face.

But from where he sat at a table, the prince remained surprisingly calm with Gilberd standing close to his side. "I understand you have a few contracts that have caught my interest. I would like to see them."

Barnaby froze mid-step, now glancing between her and Sterling. His scowl deepened as he glared at her. "You whined to the prince? Over *what* exactly? Getting a chance to wear beautiful ball gowns? Having a spouse that would regularly shower you with jewels and finery? What part of this lifestyle offends you?"

"It's not the life but the man," she replied quietly, not daring to expand on her feelings on the matter. He'd belittled her, insulted her, forced her hand, and she highly suspected him of already being unfaithful to her in their coerced betrothal. The woman wrapped in bed sheets peeking her head over the side of the stairs cinched her opinion on the matter.

"No one is accusing you of anything, Your Lordship," Sterling said in a rather diplomatic voice for a boy. "I simply wish to see the documents." He nodded toward the two soldiers. "Escort him in fetching them. Make sure he brings all of them."

But Barnaby stood his ground, arms folded. "I have nothing to prove. The contracts are unquestionably binding."

"If they are legitimately and legally binding as well as accurate, then you will have no qualms with me taking a look."

"I will not fetch them. What's done is done."

Slowly, Sterling stood and glared at him. "Do you see this man?" He nodded toward Gilberd. "He's my personal guard.

If I tell him to chop off your head, he will chop off your head." The man paled. "I suggest you do as I ask and quickly."

Gilberd's face paled as well. Surely, such a thing wasn't part of his job description.

But the threat did a thorough job of frightening Barnaby because he scrambled back up the stairs with the two soldiers practically nipping at his heels.

"You wouldn't really make me do it, would you?" Gilberd asked out of the corner of his mouth.

Sterling shook his head. "I heard my father say that once. I thought it sounded scary."

"It did," Gilberd chuckled. "It scared me, even."

The discomforting tension spiked a current of uneasiness through Mirabelle's blood as she stared at the landing, waiting for Barnaby to emerge again. Wordlessly, Gilberd took her hand, and together they shouldered the apprehension eating at her as they waited.

Only when Barnaby appeared at the top of the stairs with a flushed face did she release his hand. Because by all means, she was an engaged woman. She refused to stoop to Barnaby's level of infidelity, even if she loved Gilberd with all her heart.

"There really is no need to look at these," Barnaby insisted as he spread the documents on the table before his prince. "Everything is accurate, down to the last number. My accountants have verified the numbers multiple times. All is as it should be."

Sterling picked up one document, and then another, all while silence spread itself thin throughout the room. More than once, Barnaby glared at her, but she refused to be cowed.

But another part of her, a small part, despaired over what seemed inevitable. Sterling was just a boy. What could he possibly do without involving his father? Surely, the king would never involve himself in something so far beneath him. She was immensely lucky the prince was taking a second look at all.

"The numbers are accurate," Sterling confirmed, and her heart fell with a despondent sigh. "The wording is fair. All of the required signatures are there."

A smug grin broke through Barnaby's anxious forehead creases. "I told you it—"

"*However*," Sterling continued as he flipped one of the documents around to face Barnaby while pointing to the percentages in one of the paragraphs. "These interest rates are illegal. Private loans are legal, yes. And you could set your own rate as long as both parties agreed to it. But that was before the economy crashed." He tapped a finger against the page. "These documents should have been amended with the correct percentages when the new economic laws were passed."

Mirabelle gripped the back of a nearby chair when her legs wobbled. She hardly dared to breathe. Hardly dared to hope.

Barnaby's jaw jumped.

With a gesture of his hand, one of the two soldiers approached with a quill and ink as well as a blank parchment. Mirabelle watched as the boy's hand flew across the page with a variety of numbers and decimals, too quickly for her to follow. He finished with a number and circled it, turning it to face Barnaby once again.

"In a flourishing economy, the loan would have been paid off already. But this is how much remains of the loan with the new interest rates."

"What happened to your cattle?" Gilberd asked her, and she gripped the chair harder.

"Barnaby sold them."

"For how much?"

Her mouth twitched and her entire soul filled with relief as she nodded toward the parchment of numbers. "For more than that." She jotted the price down next to Sterling's mess of numbers, and the prince subtracted the loan money owed and circled the new amount.

"Lord Mavis," the prince gestured to the number, "you owe this family this much money. I believe this absolves Mirabelle and her mother from your debt." A flicker of uncertainty entered his eyes. "Unless you would like to keep the engagement?"

Mirabelle tore Barnaby's ring off her finger and slammed it down on the table between them. Barnaby scowled, but several layers of fear rested in his eyes, and he said nothing about the broken engagement.

"You don't have any idea what you are talking about." Barnaby pointed a finger in the prince's face. "You are just a child."

"Would you like me to take this to my father instead? I'm sure he would be interested in learning about how one of his influential subjects has been swindling good people."

By now his face lost all color. "Th-th-that isn't necessary."

Sterling clasped his hands together in his lap as if to hide the way they trembled after such a brave feat. Despite the tremors, his voice held steady. "I think reaching out to all the families that have been affected by your loans and offering apologies will be punishment enough, Your Lordship. I expect you to give them new numbers by the end of the week and repay those who have fairly paid off their loans. This includes voiding loan contracts already paid for." He nodded to Mirabelle.

With a dip of his head in a show of fealty, Barnaby murmured, "That's more than fair, Your Highness."

Barnaby dipped the quill in ink and wrote across the parchment: *Paid in full.*

Next, he reached into his coin purse and counted out what he owed Mirabelle. She pocketed the money, afraid it might disappear if she didn't take it quickly. She couldn't get her cattle back, but she had a feeling she didn't need them where she was going.

To Edilann.

The prince dipped his head in satisfaction. "You are dismissed."

Barnaby scooped up his ring and the documents and hurried back upstairs. The moment the door slammed shut, a breath stuttered out of her lungs. It was done. Finished. Paid in full. With coin to spare.

"Why did you let him off so easily?" Gilberd asked.

Sterling tucked his hands between his knees, his voice becoming quieter with the release of tension in the room. "The Mavis family comes from a long line of ancestors who have served under the Winfield rule. I can't discredit that despite how I might feel about him."

Despite their enormous gaps in stations, Mirabelle threw her arms around Sterling's shoulders and hugged him tight. He stiffened against her, but after a few moments, returned the embrace.

"Thank you, Your Highness. You don't know what you've just done for me."

He simply shrugged and swiped a hand across his nose when they broke apart. Instead of answering her, he turned toward Gilberd. "I'm ready to return home." He smiled and fiddled bashfully with the fringe on his doublet. "I think maybe I can do some good as a prince."

Gilberd beamed and squeezed his shoulder. "I know you can." And then he turned toward her, and the moment their gazes met, her stomach tied itself into knots. The man had the most beautiful eyes... "What will you do with the extra coin?"

"I don't know," she replied coyly as she fluttered her lashes at him. "Perhaps it will go toward furnishings for our new home in Edilann."

"I never—" His voice caught. "I never asked you to marry me."

"You said 'let's get married' in your letter. I believe it counts as a proposal. And my answer is yes."

Laughter escaped his mouth, and she promptly joined in when he grabbed her around the waist and spun her until she was dizzy with unobstructed joy. She felt safe in his arms, like it was where she was meant to be all along.

Her entire being melted when he bent down and closed the space between them. Their lips met in a rush of relief, of longing, of forever. She didn't need ballgowns and jewels and status. All she ever needed was him and only him.

She was exactly where she wanted to be.

16

Rice rained over their heads as Gilberd and Mirabelle descended the chapel steps, fingers tightly interlocked with nothing able to tear them apart again. Joyous laughter escaped his mouth when his new mother-in-law placed a wreath of flowers over each of their heads. He reckoned he looked ridiculous with the adornment, but he didn't care. All that mattered...

Was his beautiful wife.

An unbridled smile stretched across Mirabelle's face, a joy in her eyes to mirror his own. Ten years ago, he'd never imagined he would kneel at the altar with *Mirabelle Waters*, the girl with the double braids, stubborn mouth, and bare feet. He loved her with his entire being, and he planned to take good care of her heart for as long as he lived.

Applause, excited shouts, and whistles lifted into air, which only grew louder when he held up their intertwined fingers to show off Mirabelle's wedding band. It was a simple gold band fitted snugly to her ring finger, but the way she cherished the simple declaration of his love and commitment to her warmed his entire heart and soul.

He, on the other hand, wore her father's old ring to keep her family close in their marriage. Along with the ring, they planned to cart the man's dining table all the way to Edilann to become the first piece of furniture they decorated their home with. Her mother would live with them, journeying to Edilann only after he and Mirabelle worked out all the finer details of their living situation.

Although quieter than the rest of the excited audience, Sterling beamed at them from where he stood near the middle of the crowd between his two guards, appearing legitimately pleased with his happiness. Gilberd couldn't have asked for a better charge to watch over. Sterling was already an incredible prince, and some day, he would make an unforgettable king.

Thunder rolled across the sky, crackling with the promise of a downpour. Raindrops fell sparsely from thick, dark clouds and dotted the landscape. And as if someone smashed the clouds like a hammer against an anvil, rain poured suddenly in thick sheets.

Beside him, Mirabelle shrieked with laughter, and he couldn't help but join in when his hair became plastered against his forehead. Rainwater soaked into the ground, and dirt quickly became mud.

Wedding guests cried out and darted for shelter. Children laughed around them, running about with handfuls of mud and throwing them at one another. Gilberd couldn't help but notice how Sterling watched the mud fight longingly.

He scooped a handful into his own hands and lobbed it at one of the children, mud splattering against his back. The boy spun around and leveled an accusing stare at Prince Sterling.

"Get him!" the boy shouted, and with a chorus of war cries, the children now attacked Sterling with handfuls of mud. The prince flinched at first but then laughed as he retaliated. Just for one more day, Sterling could be a boy and not just a prince.

"What do you think?" Gilberd asked, raising an eyebrow as he glanced toward the sky. "Good luck or bad?"

His wife wrapped her arms around his neck and pulled him close, her breath flirting with his lips. "Definitely good," she murmured while twirling his hair around her finger. "I can't think of any way it could be better."

A mischievousness rested in his smirk as he pulled her closer by the waist until her body was flush against his. "Oh, I can think of one way it could be better."

Excitement squeezed his chest as she traced his bottom lip with her finger. "The barn loft is swept *and* empty. Or there is always the roof. No one will notice we're gone."

"We're the bride and groom. Of course, someone will notice." He smiled and shook his head but didn't fight her as she took his hand, and their laughter echoed in his ears as they ran down the road, their shoes flinging mud in their wake as they hurried toward her barn.

They stopped, breathless in the doorway where rainwater dripped from their hair and clothing. Gilberd ran his hands over her dark strands, along her shoulders, and down her back until he held her close by the waist with one hand, and the fingers of his other hand tangled in her hair. His wife. His smart, lovely, beautiful wife.

He slipped her sleeve to the side just enough to kiss her shoulder, then her neck, and he pulled her into a lingering kiss when he needed to taste her, to breathe her air, to make her his in mind, body, and soul.

"No roofs," he said as he kissed her ear, and then her jaw.

She laughed and threaded her fingers through his hair, igniting a fire in his belly with her touch. "Then we will just have to settle for the loft. What a shame."

"Yes, such a shame."

Their kisses paused momentarily as they rested their foreheads together, basking in the moment of their happiness. For years, he thought he would have no future other than to live, work, and die at the inn. But now he had a present and a future that was all his, one he could share with the love of his life.

"You are mine," Mirabelle whispered as she gazed at him with immense love in her eyes, love he could feel to the bottom of his soul. "Forever."

He smiled and kissed her again. "I can live with that."

BONUS CONTENT FROM

Yours, Sterling

STERLING WINFIELD'S HEART momentarily ceased beating as he laid eyes on a beautiful woman across the ballroom. Elegant honey-brown waves draped down her back, brushing against a blue and green ball gown with a bodice that pushed everything up quite nicely, tapered at a slim waist, and dripped to the floor like shimmering water.

The woman moved gracefully across the dance floor with her partner, blue eyes shining radiantly and her smile tying his stomach in knots. Her fingers... Her wrists... Her arms... They moved with a natural-born elegance, as if she had slipped dancing from the womb.

Her partner twirled her in the middle of the room, and his breath hitched at the way she seemed to float on air as her skirt fanned out around her. She was a shining star. A sparkling moon. A whisper of beauty on a breath of wind.

"That's Kathleen de Clare," his guard Gilberd said a step behind him, startling him out of his daze, "if you care to know."

"I wasn't looking at her," he defended, but even then, his gaze refused to tear itself away from her lithe form.

After a few moments, Gilberd continued, "She's the daughter of an esteemed businessman, the eldest of five sisters. And..." The man paused for dramatic effect. "She's unattached."

An anxious breath stuttered from his lungs as he continued to watch her practically float across the room. He'd never seen anyone more beautiful in his life.

Kathleen de Clare...

"Ask her to dance." Gilberd gently nudged his arm, but Sterling bit his lip with uncertainty. "You outrank her partner. He'll be forced to give her up."

Still, he hesitated.

"How do you know who she is?"

"I know who everyone is. It's my job."

"How old is she?"

"Eighteen."

Two years older than him. He was sixteen but he might as well be thirteen.

He crossed his arms, hugging himself tight around the waist. Kathleen would never look twice at him. He had yet to have a growth spurt, so she was likely taller than him. He hadn't seen a single hair on his face or chest to indicate he was on the path to manhood. And he feared witnessing a look of disappointment or disdain on her face should he ask her for a dance.

His admiration transitioned into wistful longing. Years ago, he had despised the very mention of marriage. But now? Now he realized it was a stake a claim or lose what you want kind of game. His parents gave him the freedom to choose who he wanted as a bride, warning him that if he didn't make a decision within the next two years, they would make it for him.

"What is she like?" he asked quietly, not wanting to bring attention to himself. Though, judging by several people glancing in his direction, he reckoned he made quite the stir with a crown sitting atop his head, the only royal to make an appearance at the event. The other guests only stayed their distance because Gilberd had not given them permission to approach. Not yet.

"Uh…well…" Gilberd cleared his throat, and the hesitation drew Sterling's focus from Kathleen to his guard. "She is extroverted, loves the outdoors, she enjoys painting and riding, and from what I've heard from castle gossip, she's looking for a husband."

"Then what are all of your dramatics about? What's wrong with her?"

"Nothing is wrong with her. She just…has a reputation for a quick temper."

"Is that all?"

The guard cleared his throat again and scratched his bearded cheek. "She is also known for her long trail of broken-hearted suitors. To put it into words, she is ruthless when she wants to be."

"Ah."

Kathleen seemed to possess many great qualities for a future queen. Painting took patience. The love of outdoors and riding suggested a love of adventure. An extroverted ruler would be a great asset to securing allies and friendships. A quick temper, he thought he could live with. But the possibility of rejection should he try to stake a claim?

He glanced down at himself and frowned. Wooing the woman was not currently an option. His crown might entice her. But his physical appearance? It might send her running.

But a lot could happen in two or three years in regard to his growth. By the time he was ready to marry, perhaps he might look the part of worthy suitor rather than boyish fancy.

The song ended, and Kathleen dipped into a curtsy, several strands of her hair falling to the side to reveal the smooth, flawless skin of her neck. Her partner took her hand and kissed her fingers. More than anything, he wished to be the one taking her hand and leading her in a dance, her lovely eyes captivated by his own.

He couldn't help but watch as she returned to her group of friends, each giggling and speaking in hushed whispers to one another. When a song started up, another man asked Kathleen for a dance and whisked her across the room, this time behind several couples to shroud her from his vision.

Kathleen was a popular dance partner. He didn't doubt she was highly sought after in courtship as well.

Nearby, he overheard a group of men laughing and jesting with one another. One of them swirled the liquid in his glass and eyed Kathleen in a slightly different manner than himself, with lust in his eyes rather than admiration.

"Then why aren't you dancing with her, Lord Rupert?" One of the men laughed and punched him in the shoulder so amber liquid spilled out of his glass.

"I am practically engaged to the woman," Lord Rupert replied. "I don't need to dance with her. I know where I stand. Surely, her father will agree to the match."

Sterling balled his hands into fists when he realized just how sought after Kathleen was. If he didn't act. He would lose his chance altogether.

Curses!

He had no choice but to face her in a body that wasn't quite ready for her. At least he found a measure of satisfaction in knowing she couldn't turn away his advances in a room full of onlookers. His station as heir to a throne far outranked not only her but her dance partner as well. It would save his pride should she find him lacking.

Unless she truly was as ruthless as Gilberd seemed to think she was.

Taking a deep breath, he steeled his nerves and dug deep within himself for the courage he needed to face this beautiful, elegant, flower-breathing dragon. He took one step onto the dance floor, and then another, until he found himself weaving in and out of dancing couples.

However, when people started to notice him, the couples moved out of the way, creating a path for him as they watched his movements. Kathleen was only two couples away now…

Something slammed into him, and he crashed onto the floor, landing hard on his elbows. His crown skittered across the ground, but before he could reach it in his momentary daze, someone snatched it up and helped him to his feet.

"Forgive me, Prince Sterling," the man said as he guided him to the side of the dance floor while handing back his crown. "It's my fault. I didn't see you."

The blue of the man's eyes looked familiar, and with a start, he realized they looked similar to Kathleen's. "What is your name?"

"Theodore de Clare, Your Highness."

The hope of good fortune alighted in his chest as he placed the crown back onto his head and straightened it over his brow. "And did you bring anyone with you tonight?"

The man nodded and gestured with a hand toward the dance floor. "My eldest daughter, Kathleen, and my second eldest, Millie. Both are officially out in society."

Sterling glanced over his shoulder to find Gilberd slowly edging along the ballroom, somehow managing to move about unseen despite his large stature. He couldn't wait for his guard to catch up. He needed to take advantage of this opportunity immediately.

"May I speak to you privately?"

A seriousness lined Theodore's pinched mouth as if fearing retribution for knocking him to the ground. Still, he gave him a forced smile. "Of course. I believe there are a few rooms just down the hallway."

He followed the older man out of the ballroom, down a hallway, and into an empty room, closing the door behind them. Mr. de Clare lit a lamp, lighting a small library in a warm glow.

For what seemed like once in his life, he didn't feel anxiety over his physical insecurities. Because he knew what he wanted, and he was determined to get it. To get *her*. "I know this is sudden, but…I would like to marry your daughter, Kathleen de Clare."

Theodore froze as if taken aback by his request. The man's gaze dragged from his toes to the top of his head. "Please do not take this the wrong way, Your Highness. But have you…come of age?"

"Well…" He scratched the back of his neck. "I will be of age in two years. However, I know of engagements that have lasted far longer." He pretended to fix a crooked crown if only to draw the man's attention to it. "I am next in line to become King of Edilann. Kathleen would be a queen. What's two years in comparison to a lifetime in an influential position of power?"

A long breath escaped Theodore's lips as he leaned back against the desk and stared at him, his gaze far away as if deep in thought. After what felt like the longest time, Sterling thought he wouldn't say anything. But finally, the man spoke.

"I am a businessman, Prince Sterling. I can recognize a good, fair deal when I see it." He unfolded his arms and nodded. "I agree to a tentative betrothal. When you come of age, you and my daughter will marry. But *only* if we have not received a better offer for her hand."

What could possibly be better than the promise of a king? Or future king, for that matter? Therefore, Sterling held out his hand and the two of them shook on the deal.

"Just between you and I, if you will," Theodore said with his mouth pinched once again. "I do not want this to become public knowledge until it is made official in two years. Allow my daughter to enjoy the next two years with friendships and suitors and whatever else might make her happy."

Sterling grinded his teeth together at the thought of Kathleen courting anyone other than him. "I do not believe this is how betrothals work, Mr. de Clare. Either we are engaged, or we are not."

"I think it's more than fair. If you will have her wait two years for you, then you must allow her to grow and thrive as anyone her age ought to. I will turn away suitors who try to get too serious. Unless I see a better offer in them, of course."

Unfortunately, Sterling recognized the wisdom in the man's words. Who was he to deprive Kathleen two years' worth of happiness while waiting on a sixteen-year-old fiancé to grow up? Sterling wasn't ready to court her. Not yet. Not like this. But he knew without a doubt he wanted to marry her, so therefore, he was staking his claim.

"Then I am hoping to become one of those suitors in the coming months." They shook hands once more. "I agree to keep the betrothal a secret for now. But I expect you to remain good on your word."

"I swear I will. I am a fair and honest businessman and never go back on my word."

Sterling exited the room, only to find Gilberd standing against the wall several doors away down the hallway. If he knew what went on behind the closed door, he said nothing as Sterling passed and returned to the ballroom.

But then his heart squeezed painfully tight when Kathleen exited at the same time with her friend at her side. They bumped shoulders, close enough for him to capture the flowery scent wafting from her hair.

She giggled with an elegant hand covering her mouth and dipped into a curtsy. "Pardon me." She glanced at his crown and smiled. "Your Highness."

He stared at her smiling mouth and his heart stuttered at the beautiful sound of her laughter as she carried on her way. He begged himself to call after her, to speak to her, to ask her for a dance. But he only managed to stare dumbstruck, admiring the way she moved, the way her skirts swished around her, the way her voice captured his soul like an enrapturing melody.

"Kingdom's glory," Gilberd muttered behind him. "You are in trouble, Sterling."

The spell broken, he turned and scowled at his guard. "Not a word, Gilberd. Not a word."

And then Kathleen disappeared around the corner, a breath of longing escaping his mouth with her sudden absence. Two years couldn't come soon enough.

ABOUT THE AUTHOR

Sydney Winward is an award-winning fantasy and paranormal romance author who dabbles in the occasional historical fiction. She loves building complex worlds filled with magic, strong characters, and emotional stories that can make you laugh and cry.

Sydney is the author of the Sunlight and Shadows Series and the best-selling Bloodborn Series, and when she's not writing, she's reading, thinking about stories, or going on adventures with her children. She lives in Utah with her husband, two amazing kids, and one stubborn fish.

www.sydneywinward.com